Babylon's Fall

M. R. Black

*For my husband,
without whom I may never have emerged
from the chrysalis that was created for me.*

Liache watches me from the door as I place a little pill of God knows what in my mouth and swallow it. Finally, she's ready to leave. Her green eyes are lined heavily in black, brown curls pinned back haphazardly out of her face; her little black dress highlights all the right curves.

She turns her back to me and glances flirtatiously over her shoulder. "Zip me up?"

I get up, walk toward her, and zip up her dress on our way out the door.

She drives me to the venue and helps the roadies set up the last of everything. She wants it to be perfect for me because she's my angel.

Everyone is in stage gear and makeup because it's all about showmanship with heavy metal. Gabriel, Marc, and Luc are all waiting for me, looking slightly annoyed. At least, they are until I offer them some of my drugs. That's when they remember why they keep me around.

I scream until my voice is raw on stage, and then I scream some more. The fans are screaming back, sometimes the same words and sometimes incoherently. My screaming feeds their screaming, and their screaming feeds my buzz. This is an excellent symbiotic arrangement, an unspoken agreement with no strings attached.

After our set, I spend no time on stage. I am gone within seconds. My buzz is wearing off, and I have a beautiful woman to tend to before any other creeps hiding backstage can talk to her.

I trust her completely, and it's these heady lead singers for other bands I don't trust. Being a vocalist takes a particular ego, attitude, and selfishness. Most people in the industry have questionable motives at best.

I find Liache and pin her against the wall, kissing her forcefully. Her reaction, how she melts in my embrace, tells me she belongs to me, and I need to display that prominently. After letting her go, she laughs, handing me the drugs I've been after. I smile at her and go through the door, rejoining my men.

We're at home. I'm not sure how we got here, but it doesn't matter. Liache is with me, and we're walking through the front door. Bedroom door? The lights inside the house dance with joy in more colors than I can count around us as we walk through, highlighting everything in a warm glow. Liache is holding my hand, leading me into a bright abyss. Everything looks so soft. She throws me onto one surface or another and climbs on top of me, kissing my face, neck, and chest as what seems to be soft, fluffy clouds envelop us. I tell her I want her; she tells me she knows. I tell her I need her, and she smiles and laughs. We spend the night in passion, and after she falls asleep, I slip out of the house.

    I walk through the forest surrounding our home, still naked because what's the point of getting dressed? There's nobody out here. The dancing lights of unfathomable colors have morphed into troublesome little fairies, bouncing around and flirting with danger, illuminating a path and leading me to God knows where. Everything is bright and cheerful for a while.

    The further I get from my house, the darker everything seems. The trees become twisted and gnarly, and the fairies' glow dimmer, getting lost in a dark, thick, swirling fog. But then, after some more time has passed, I realize there are voices all around me talking about me. Dreary, melancholy voices close in on me in this wilderness. They mutter, wondering if I know, whispering about who I truly am, what I'm destined to be. But, of course, I know, I've always known.

    I try to keep going, but the voices get so loud, and the forest gets so dark and terrifying that I must stop. I break down and hit my knees, screaming.

    Sometimes I wonder if I'm supernaturally sensitive or just absolutely insane. Sometimes I wonder if I'm holding Liache back from more extraordinary things. Still, I remember that she was made for me and will rise to fame with me.

    Liache must have found me because the next thing I can remember is being inside the house, looking for more drugs.

    I don't know what day it is, and I don't particularly care. I know I don't have another show for a while, and I'm happy with that. There's nothing more frustrating than obligations, regardless of my love for performing.

    Liache has gone to her father's house to visit for the day,

and obviously, that means I've reacted much like a puppy, sure she's never going to come home to me. So, I'm scouring the house for drugs. Anything I can find goes into my mouth or nose without hesitation, with no discrimination.

I'm wandering the forest again, wondering exactly how I got this far from the house. I love living here. It's quiet, private--this forest goes on for miles and miles with nobody around. We might as well live in the wilderness with all the amenities of modern living. It's so beautiful here.

This is one of the rare times I'm out here like this in the day. The sun is shining through the leaves of these gorgeous deciduous trees, casting an emerald green light on everything. I can see leprechauns scurrying about, trying not to be seen. They don't know that I'm not going to bother them. The dust and pollen in the air make this place look like a fairy tale. And it might as well be, the way I'm seeing it. Fairies are flying around me, for once not bothering me, not flying in my face, or trying to poke out my eyes, and I'm sure this is heaven on Earth.

There's so much softened light diffused by hundreds of thousands of leaves and so much beauty that it swells my heart. I love the smell of this forest, the sight of the sunshine filtering in through everything, the life--real and hallucination--that thrives here at this very moment. I believe God has blessed me with this moment, guiding me back home.

A gust of wind sweeps through, blowing thousands of dandelion seeds into the air. Across my vision, they float as one, swept up by the same breeze and dispersed into the ether, to eventually settle and sprout their weeds—thousands of wishes.

There is an innocence here I've never known. I don't know anything about what I've done and how my actions have affected people. So, I go on my day-to-day routine selfishly, not realizing there is more to life than survival and self-destruction.

But that doesn't mean I'm going to change. That doesn't make me self-aware. It barely even makes me human.

I know now that I am a monster and that Liache's perfection demands more, but I can't bring myself to do anything about it now. I'm too deep into adolescent self-loathing. I've been too deep into adolescent self-loathing for over a decade now. I'm crazy; I'm addicted; I'm imperfect and flawed. I am the demon to her angel; I am darkness, mourning, and pain. And for now, that's alright.

I find the small lake somewhere in the middle of this forest and sit at its edge, resting my feet in the water as I marvel at the reflection of the light and trees on the water. There's more life under the surface that I can't see, and I want to desperately, but I know better than going into this lake in my state right now.

Eventually, I see the reflection of Liache coming to sit down beside me. I wonder idly how long I've been out here.

"I've been looking for you," she says. "I was worried I'd lost you."

I smile at her, and I know she can tell I'm high. I know she doesn't care, but I know she will eventually.

"You'll never lose me, Liache," I respond romantically. "I could never walk away from you."

She laughs at my truth, and I laugh with her. I'm a giant cheese ball, but I can't help it. I love her. I doubt I'll ever tell her those words, but I love her, and she knows it without saying it.

The problem with it is that my love is destructive. My love is self-absorbed and painful and corrosive. My love is poison.

Liache kisses my cheek and rests her head on my shoulder, looking out across the lake at the expanse of trees, through it with me as I muse gently on how perfect this moment is. It's so perfect it's making me suspicious. It's too quiet, too lovely, too bright. It's so happy; these things don't happen in my life. I won't allow them, but I can't help but wonder what is coming next and what I can expect to mess up my calm. Liache can sense this, and she squeezes my hand gently.

"It's okay to be happy."

She always knows what I need to hear. I nudge her head with my cheek to look up, kissing her passionately. I love how she smells, tastes, and exists in perfection. She's always consummately in harmony with life, with nature. She is elegance and light; she is love and purity. She is my angel, made special for me.

She leans into the kiss, egging me until we make love in this soft bed of leaves and grass, sheltered from life by the gorgeous foliage.

We are our fairy tale. We are perfect opposites. I am the darkness to her light, the cruelty to her kindness, the selfishness to her graciousness. And honestly, I wouldn't have it any other way because she belongs to me this way.

Liache tells me she loves me, whispering it into my ear, and I kiss her forehead in response, unable to say the words. If I admit I love her, I'm bound to hurt her. That is a truth I cannot handle. She deserves better than my pain; she deserves better than to have my essence caustically assault her.

I get up and walk back to the house, knowing she will follow. It is dark now, and I'm sure there are bugs, but I don't care.

When I look back, there is some distance between her and me, and a shadow begins to take shape in that distance. It is significant, corporeal, and terrifying. In my eyes, it becomes a great monster chasing me down.

Without hesitation, I dart off, not paying attention to the direction I'm going in as the creature gives chase. As it gains on me, approaching me from behind at an alarming rate, I leap up, grabbing a low branch, hauling myself up into the tree's boughs. I climb as high as possible before branches break, just out of the monster's reach. I hear Liache calling after me, and so does the shadow. As Liache approaches, trying to calm me down, I realize suddenly that this creature is just the manifestation of everything that I think can go wrong between us. That realization is every bit as terrifying as the actual creature.

Liache stands at the bottom of the tree, and the monster disappears, dispersing like a cloud of smoke as her natural light breaks through.

"You have got to stop taking that drug," she says, trying to calm her heart rate.

I climb down and hug her but say nothing. We walk back to the house, hand in hand, and I realize that I'm terrible for holding onto this when I know it's slowly destroying her. I know it's killing her to watch me wreck myself and self-destruct daily. What makes me worse is that I don't care. Nothing matters to me if I have her.

We crawl into bed together, and I can feel the incredible softness of her skin against mine as I wrap my arms around her. Before long, Liache is asleep, and I'm left wide awake, thinking about how terrible I am, how I'm torturing her, and how it's not fair that this was her purpose in life. It's almost as if she's made just to endure my bullshit, destruction, and insanity.

Eventually, I can feel my breathing deepen, my heart rate slow, and my eyelids become heavy as I go into a blissfully deep sleep.

I slept so soundly that I didn't even notice Liache get up for her art class. What woke me was a jarring, terrifying sensation as my bed was lifted at least two feet from the end and dropped heavily back onto the floor. I sit up at once, gasping for air as my heart explodes. I see Gabriel, tall and built like a brick shit house, standing at the end of my bed with Marc and Luc on either side.

"Get the fuck up and get dressed," he barks, not bothering with any explanation.

Disgruntled, I oblige. I scowl at them and get up, not bothering to cover my shame as I walk past them. Of course, I have no idea what's happening, only that they seem upset. Not a smile, not a joke, faces as severe as if someone's mother had died. I wonder what's going on as I follow them out to the car; they all came in.

I sit shotgun as Gabriel drives, Marc and Luc seated in the back seat. Eventually, it is Luc who breaks the silence.

"Dude, what the hell 'ave you been doing for the past month?" he asks, confusion and concern evident in his voice.

I don't know what he's talking about, and I tell him as much. As far as I know, it was only a few days ago that we played a show together.

Marc scoffs, "it's been a month since then," he explains. "We called you, but Liache kept telling us you were sleeping or running errands."

I'm confused, and Gabriel continues driving. He knew exactly what I was doing. He knows better than to buy into my crap, and suddenly I understand why they're all here.

There's nearly ten minutes more of silence before Marc

speaks up again.

"She loves you more dan anyt'ing, you know," he says quietly, nothing more than a disembodied voice floating somewhere behind my head. "She takes care of you, and that's 'uge."

"She does everything for you, bro," Luc pipes up. "And she does it because you clearly can't care for yourself."

Gabriel continues driving, his stony silence having more impact on me than anything Marc and Luc are saying. I rest my head against the window's glass and peer out as the trees become sparser, and it is buildings that begin to fly past.

Life looks so monotonous now. The colors seem muted, and that's only amplified by the dull, diffused light of the sun, filtering through heavy clouds. There are no bright lines, no colorful hallucinations, and absolutely nothing of note. Life is boring, and I realize that the only absolute truth is that we all die. But not all of us are damned, and life is only fun for those who are damned if we're making it so.

That's why there are performers, artists, musicians, comedians, painters, and illustrators; we are the damned. We are cursed with the intelligence to see and dissect everyday life and recognize the patterns of distraction in politics, social justice, gossip, reality television, and the news for what they are. Just a distraction from the mortality that we all must face someday. But it doesn't change that we are terrified of our ultimate demise.

Gabriel stops the car. He hasn't said a word since he woke me up, and that's more than a bit concerning, considering he is the largest man in our band—both in height and muscle.

The morning light reflects off his sunglasses as I watch him walk around the front of the car to the passenger side door and open it. The fabric of my shirt bunches at his fist as he lifts me out of the vehicle and places me on my feet in front of him. A second of confusion clear on my face before I feel unimaginable pain as his massive fist connects with my cheekbone. Then, all I see is white as the momentum from his punch forces my head to turn, taking the rest of my body with it. Life seems to go in slow motion as I fall to the ground. My elbow scrapes the pavement, and my other hand struggles and misses me.

Pain radiates across the left side of my face, spreading to the rest of my head. I squint my left eye closed as my body struggles to understand what happened.

Gabriel doesn't give me a chance to recover. Instead, he lifts me again and places me on my feet in front of him.

"How do you feel about Liache?" he asks sternly, anger bubbling below the surface.

I look at him sideways, through one squinted eye and constricted pupils. "She's my angel."

"Then start fucking treating her that way." This is all Gabriel says. The lecture is over; the pain I feel is just his version of an exclamation point. He has made his argument incredibly clear.

This is an intervention of some sort, but not where my friends take me to a rehab center. And I'm alright with that. Anything that can help me avoid taking responsibility for my actions is good.

It takes me a moment to realize where we are, but I understand why they are so frustrated when I do. Yes, they are concerned about Liache, and they want me to stop being a jerk, take care of her, and start treating her the way she deserves, but they're also frustrated because, in that month, I haven't shown up for her any practice or recording sessions. They know me better than to try to appeal to me for their best interests or even my own. They know that my ego feeds itself whatever it needs to, but they also know nothing I wouldn't do for Liache.

They feed me drugs, just enough to wake me up, and we head into our practice hall. I'm rusty, but getting back into the groove is good. We are there until the sun sets, and we have several new songs written. Gabriel drives me home in complete silence and talks to Liache for a few minutes when we get there. I pay little attention to them, at least until he hugs her.

I'm walking past the doorway to the kitchen when I spot them. My head turns and stops moving, but my feet forget. Ultimately, I'm peeking around the corner, leering at them like a complete asshole as Gabriel waves at me. I wave back, and he walks out of the door; Liache, meanwhile, is staring at me like I'm a lunatic. She shakes her head dismissively and walks into the kitchen behind me. My eyes follow her like magnets.

She's so perfect. She is the picture of beauty, nature's finest work, and she's mine. She belongs to me. And Gabriel is right; I need to start treating her properly, proving to her that she's important to me. At least I can say that I've never cheated on her. I may be a mess and hate myself, but I don't hate myself enough to destroy the only relationship worth anything in my life.

I pour us both shots of vodka as she cooks dinner. Delicious, savory aromas fill our home as we take one vile, tasteless, burning shot of alcohol after another, our faces flushing and voices climbing in volume as we do what we do best; imbibe intoxicants.

Dinner is fantastic, flavorful, and gone. I can barely even remember what it was, just that it was delectable. Across the table, we laugh and joke, play, and throw food at each other. Before long, we are slow dancing in our kitchen. No music is playing, but that doesn't stop us from rocking in each other's arms. Liache's head is against my chest, and all I can smell is her wonderful scent.

I can almost feel our souls dancing in time with us, wanting desperately to be the same, be one, and fight against their very nature.

This is how she knows I love her without saying it: this ethereal communication, this moment, this intangible feeling. I have spent over five years trying to give her everything she wants, working towards setting up myself in the media, the country, and the world, and it's paying off now. And I've done it all so that she will never have to work a day in her life.

Liache kisses me gently, and I lift her. With her legs wrapped around my waist, I carry her carefully to our room as the precious gift that she is. We don't need words; we barely need actions; we just know.

For the first time in my life, I can just enjoy the moment and not be suspicious, worried, or making up some bullshit; I'm not allowing myself to ruin the perfection that is this moment. I'm worshiping Liache as she's meant to be for the first time.

For the first time, there's hope for me.

Of course, as with everything in my life, my hopefulness doesn't last very long. Within a couple of weeks, I'm back to the same old me, finding something to gripe about in everything and generally being self-piteous.

I've forgotten what I've taken, but I'm sitting in the boughs of a large tree, chain-smoking cigarettes and watching pixies and fairies fight in the leaves overhead. There's nothing more to this now than maybe a slight depression coupled with my addiction.

People keep telling me hallucinogens aren't addictive, but I beg to differ. When you embody apathy, see more extraordinary, grander things, and understand life's blessing on a level that others cannot understand, hallucinogens are the only way to experience life.

I am destruction; I am death, I am...

"Get down from there, you son of a bitch!"

...not half as badass as I think I am.

I look over to where Liache's voice is coming from and sigh. I was hiding. It doesn't happen often, but I know that sometimes, I get too self-obsessed even for Liache to handle.

I try to get down gracefully but snagged on the bottom bough, hanging from my knees before falling onto my shoulders. It takes me a second to catch my breath, but Liache looms over me, her brows furrowed.

"You have shit to do," she says, earnestly trying to get me to understand responsibility as if I'm capable of worrying about anything other than myself. "Get to Gabriel's now; you guys have work to do."

Even when she's upset with me, she's thinking of my best interest, a blessing, and a curse. She enables me to be this way, to hurt myself like this, but it's only because it's all she's ever known of me, and she fell in love with me anyway.

She doesn't realize how intoxicated I am, but I oblige, somehow making it over to Gabriel's.

When I arrive, there are only the two of us there. Gabriel nods at me, suggesting that we're waiting on Luc and Marc. Which is fine; it's all fine. It doesn't matter anyway because Gabriel and I do more of it than they do regarding creation. I swat at what I think is a fly buzzing around my head but realize that there's absolutely nothing there shortly after Gabriel looks at me like I'm insane.

The room pulses and quivers, and I have finally figured out that I hadn't even hit the peak of my trip on whatever I took before I left. I have no idea how I'm going to get home.

I try to sit on the couch, inconspicuous as always, but trip over the morphing floor and land flat on my face, a few inches from Gabriel's coffee table.

"Did you drive here like that?" he asks quietly. There's no emotion behind his voice, no real judgment, nothing at all.

I dust myself off, sitting heavily on the couch that won't stop moving.

"I wasn't this bad yet," I respond, matching his tone. It's difficult for me to act normal now; this is different from usual. Everything feels... fuzzy.

"Whatever, it's not like you write anything good while you're sober anyway," Gabriel jabs as he looks up from the paper he's writing on to smile at me. He doesn't care if I live or die outside his little world; it would make his road to Liache clearer.

I shut down that thought as it occurs. I can't afford to think like that right now; I need happy thoughts.

Marc and Luc burst through the door of Gabriel's house in a grand show of energy and volume. Sometimes, it's clear that they are brothers.

They rain down in a shower of drugs and hugs and are willing to share. Eventually, though, Marc and Luc are plucking away, sitting in the two chairs on either side of the couch, Marc playing his bass and Luc his guitar, as Gabriel and I feverishly set to work, creating the way we are best at creating.

We bounce ideas off each other, nodding in agreement or offering advice here or there while simultaneously getting wildly excited when Marc or Luc hits something we want to use.

It is hectic and not how most people do it, but this is how we work together.

It helps that we've all known one another for years. This is one of those few times that teenage pipe dreams became a reality. We've been dying to create together for so long, and I wasn't sure if we'd ever get this far, but we managed. We fell into popularity at a shocking rate, and now we're struggling to keep up with demand.

Due to my incapability, however, we haven't been working on something for almost two months that we should have started six months ago, and we're behind schedule.

"It's fine whatever, shit, it's fine." I find myself repeating it while the boys give me a hard time over it. They need to stop insisting I lay off the drugs when they know it'll never happen. It takes me a moment to realize the only person not mocking me right now is Gabriel, and all I can hear is this deep, disembodied voice as it nags quietly in my ear. I look over to where Gabriel is sitting and see him holding a phone to his ear. Distantly, I can hear Liache on the other end. He's assuring her that I'm here, safe and that there's nothing she needs to worry about. I pull my phone out of my pocket, look down at it and realize I have 13 missed calls.

Gabriel looks at me. "Learn to answer your phone."

Craziness is swimming in my head, and now, I can see tiny versions of Gabriel and Liache in compromising and enraging positions instead of my usual fairies. I curse under my breath and return to writing.

Somewhere in the distance, I can hear our manager screaming at us about how we released dates before they were finalized and made promises before we'd even begun working on this project. You can't disappoint your fans, especially when you talk like I do. My speech has too many definitives; I don't leave any room for error. That's how I am; somehow, we always manage to pull it off. Always.

And I'm never involved in anything past the point of recording vocals. Ever.

This is why they secretly hate me. It requires much more work than I put into it, and they're left with everything else. Then again, my work makes all the money, right?

Eventually, Marc and Luc are play fighting and knock over one decoration or another. They look around like puppies caught in the middle of ripping their owner's clothing to shreds and set it back up where it belongs. It catches my attention because it's one of Liache's pieces. It was sold, legitimately sold online. I file that away because it's not important right now. And it doesn't matter if he wants her or not; she was made for me. She'll never leave.

At some point, we'll all come together and create this correctly, but right now, we have some excellent, skeletal outlines of what we want to happen to go on. It's time for me to go home because while I want to pick a fight with Gabriel, I don't think I should, at least not in this state.

The drugs I was already on have mixed with the drugs that Luc has provided for us, and I feel like it's time to stop, which means I need to remove myself from the situation entirely. I don't have the strength to stop on my own. Gabriel can tell, as he always can, and he tells Liache to come and get me. It's OK; my car will still be here tomorrow.

It is a quiet ride home with my Liache. She seems too tired to spend tonight chasing me around like she usually does, and that's fine. She deserves a rest. I lay in bed with her and rub her back until she falls asleep.

Of course, as always, I sneak away and wander through the forest. What else am I supposed to do until all these drugs wear off?

I have this running theory that people don't like to see photos of themselves or videos or hear recordings of their voices because there's audacity in it. The pictures, videos, and recordings mean that you had to have existed for them to now exist. There's an ego they don't like to feed. They don't want to believe they are attractive or talented or worth remembering.

I love my voice. I love my face. I love seeing the videos we make and hearing the music we play. I hate myself more than anybody else, yet my ego is so gigantic that I love the proof that I exist. And nothing excites me more than the idea of thousands of screaming fans; nothing piques my interest so much as how many women wish they were Liache.

I couldn't care less about them, and I would certainly never give in to their fantasies because that would mean giving someone else what they wanted, and that's unacceptable, but the fact that they're there; that's delectable. And I know that on some level, Liache loves it too. She gets to have what so many others want, and only she gets it.

I'm back in my tree, chain-smoking in the darkness of night, struggling to see the stars through the canopy of dark leaves overhead.

I can feel the smoke curling down my throat in my weakened state, infecting every alveolus, crawling into every crevasse. I watch in wonder as I exhale, and it all rises towards the heavens, curling upwards like great, carcinogenic claws. I laugh, take another cigarette, and hang peacefully in this tree until the sun's first dim light creeps into my skewed view of the sky.

The sky is a blazing, painful shade of red for a few moments. It almost looks like the atmosphere is on fire ,like God himself decided that he'd had enough of our heathen ways. Like Sodom, like Gomorrah, threatening to swallow our civilization into fire and brimstone. I know that's not true, but it sets me on edge anyway.

I have long since stopped hallucinating, and I'm not sure if there are remaining drugs still keeping me awake or just too deep in thought to bother trying to sleep. I don't need Liache right now; I don't need anybody. For once, I'm complete on my own.

The sun rises higher in the sky, and I can see the clouds creeping in as the day breaks. It's going to rain. The air is heavy with moisture, and I can smell the impending dampness. I struggle internally as to whether I should go inside. I love the rain.

I climb out of the tree more gracefully than usual and walk back into the house. I climb back into bed beside Liache, and I can feel her moving closer. I close my eyes to sleep and find that it's jot happening. I guess I'm just going to lay awake next to Liache until she wakes up.

She was frustrated with me yesterday, but today is a new day; I saw the dawn, and it was beautiful. She'll love me more today; I know it.

I watch as she sleeps, how her dark brown hair has been disheveled in the night, the remnants of her mascara have spread and smeared beneath her eyes, and her gentle, rhythmic breathing is deep and relaxed. She is so pale, but I can see the faint hints of freckles across her cheeks, where they would be if she ever

14

ventured outside during the day. When she wakes, I will be met with eyes of emeralds, with a depth that seems to go on forever. I kiss her cheek in gentle musings, and her skin is like fire against my lips. It always seems that way to me.

There's some hyperactivity to my senses. Everything is either way too much or not nearly enough. I find myself drowning in everything around me or dying of a severe thirst for my emotion.

Over the next several weeks, the boys and I finish putting together an entire album. Written, recorded, and printed. They've been setting up for a tour, something I'm always on the fence about.

Liache knows I can handle myself, to an extent anyway. She doesn't need to worry about me and anybody else, so she's fine staying at home when we go on tour. Correction: she insists on staying home when we go on tour. She has her classes, and she doesn't want to miss them. But I have a hard time being away from her.

I don't need to worry about that for several months, though. That's a problem for future me.

I need to worry about everything we have set up to promote the tour. I need to prepare for these interviews for magazines and radio stations, solidifying our image and our place in the media. That means that I need to be mostly sober for these; I need to have the answers to the questions. I need not be swatting at invisible creatures.

Easy enough, right?

It's a mere few hours until the first interview I'm to do—magazine-style, the kind that is easiest to handle. Nothing is live; no need to watch my tongue or worry about the audience's sensibility. The readers of these magazines usually know what they're getting into. This isn't my first rodeo, however much it may seem to be.

Today, I'm picking Liache up from her art class. Or at least I got the car from our house to the studio after doing the rest of the drugs I had in my possession.

As I sit, waiting and smoking a cigarette, I realize that I

15

was sober while driving compared to what's happening to me now. I feel as if I'm still moving too fast. I wonder if Liache had been trying to keep me sober for my interview by asking me to pick her up.

People begin to pour from the studio's doors, talking and laughing among themselves like old friends at a reunion. Walking out just behind Liache is Gabriel. He walks away after saying goodbye, and she starts in the direction of my car.

When I open the car door, a rush of hot air assaults my senses; the scent of hot concrete almost chokes me as I stand and look at Liache over the roof. Things are morphing a bit in my vision, looking distorted and confused. As Liache approaches, she looks directly into my eyes, and her smile fades.

"Jesus, are you serious right now?" she asks sharply, incredulous and agitated. "You have an interview in like, an hour. Put on your stupid sunglasses and get away from the driver's seat. Now."

I smile at her, teasing her. The intense heat radiates from the blazing metal hood of the car as I run my hand along it for fear of floating off while wandering to the passenger door. I can feel the smile on my face, broad and mocking, as Liache drives towards my interview. Complete silence envelopes the space between us, and eventually, my smile fades. She is angry with me.

Her anger sits like a fog, polluting the air inside the car, threatening to steal the oxygen and suffocate us both. I can almost see red heat swirling and twisting about her dark hair and gorgeous features. I can feel the tension in my chest, what feels like an immune response to her anger and distrust.

A familiar building creeps up from a distance, and Liache stops the car in front of it.

"I will be right there," she hisses these last two words, accentuating their importance as she points to a quaint little cafe at once next to where I need to be. "Come get me when you're done."

I nod and move in for a quick kiss before I leave. She allows it but is brisk. "Don't fuck up."

The interviewers always seem particularly interested in

me, taking or leaving the other band members as they see fit. My ego says it's because the others aren't important, but in all likelihood, I'm the problem child of the group. I'm the one who can't keep my mouth shut; I'm the one on intoxicated escapades; I'm the one insulting fans to their faces and publicly flaunting my girlfriend and writing the fucking lyrics. I am the terrible influence of this generation, inspiring the cries of desperation, 'but think of the children!'

I am the drug-addled face of teenage rebellion, and I wouldn't have it any other way.

I make my way to the offices of this specific magazine, the name of which escapes me because I never cared to learn it in the first place. I find it odd that he wanted to meet with me at his office. These types of interviews are almost always done over the phone.

I look around sluggishly, barely hearing what this sudden swarm of people is saying to me as they blur around me, preparing me in a consistent blur for God knows what. The interviewer keeps me walking while people buzz around me. Someone swipes my sunglasses straight off my face; another pats me down with a soft brush. I sneeze as the powdered makeup to take the shine away floats up my nose, hilariously enough. I laugh as I entertain the idea that something so harmless could make me sneeze after all the drugs have presumably burned away any nerve endings long ago.

Slowly, and much to my chagrin, I realize this is not the magazine interview I thought when we enter a studio with bright lights and cameras. This is a taped interview for television.

I sit in the chair that they tell me to while a few others buzz around, finishing whatever they were doing, tuck my sunglasses into the collar of my shirt, and I start to panic internally.

I don't know any of this information; I've long since forgotten it. I don't know what this person will ask, and as far as I'm concerned, those bright lights are literally on fire.

Liache was right to have tried to keep me sober.

The countdown goes from 4 to silent, the cameras are rolling, and the interviewer introduces himself, the show, and me.

17

Without hesitation, he launches into his first question.

"You and the rest of your bandmates, Marc, Gabriel, and Luc, have been part of many hot-button debates among parents and, quite honestly, the school districts for quite some time. How do you find yourself dealing with this negative feedback?" His well-rehearsed question lashes forth, not surprising, but this one is simple to answer.

"Well," I ponder for a second, organizing my thoughts and praying that I don't look high. "The thing is that it doesn't directly affect us in the long run. These teenagers, and any of the fans that listen to us, well, they're going to listen to us whether or not their teachers and parents are against it. That's the beauty of being in a free country."

The interviewer smiles at me, his perfect teeth glinting in the bright light. "So, you have no retaliation to the allegations of violence being conducted on your behalf?"

"No. People will do what they're going to do, and that has nothing to do with the type of music they listen to," I respond honestly, with conviction. I sit forward and position myself more comfortably in my chair. "Look, the nicest people I have met, the kindest and most caring and gentle people, have all listened to this type of music. The lyrics, yes, are typically violent and angry and of a type of poetry that people aren't accustomed to, so I get why people think that it's my fault their children are beating each other up and swearing and being generally violent. Still, the fact of the matter is, when it's the music you listen to, you're living vicariously through somebody else, and you're not likely to go out and start punching people in the face. It's the poetry that we write, not our actions. There's a difference."

"I've never really thought about it that way," the interviewer admits. "So then, this look, the dark clothing, the makeup you wear on stage, the long black hair, is this just part of the image, or is this how you feel comfortable?"

"Are you comfortable in that suit?" I get this one a lot. I like to turn it around. For some reason, it always surprises them.

He chuckles. "Fair point. So, the contacts?"

"No, I'm not wearing contacts," I blurt pointedly. "Though my icy blue gaze lends to this creepy overall look people love to hate or hate to love, I haven't decided yet."

The interviewer nods, acknowledging my statement but refusing to respond. "So, you're going on tour soon. Can you give us any information about where you'll be and when you'll be there?"

I laugh heartily. "Fucked if I know."

He snickers back nervously. "Well, I'm sure we can find it all posted on your website." I've made him uncomfortable.

He launches into some sign-off bullshit that I don't care to pay attention to, and I just walk off the set. The cameras are still rolling, and I'm already out the door. I'm positive that he's still wrapping up by the time I reach the sidewalk outside. I don't care. I just want to get back to Liache, like I always do.

I know I won't remember the interview at all. It's only been a few minutes, and I already can't remember what I said. I never knew the guy's name. That's not new; I never bother to remember anybody's name.

Hot, dry air rushes past me as I bust open the double glass doors at the entrance of the building, sunglasses firmly in place as the world swirls around me in technicolor. I laugh and waltz across the street to where Liache said she would be, and there she was indeed. Gabriel sits at a table outside, laughing and drinking what I can only assume is a fancy latte infused with almond-jizz.

Seriously? How much time can he spend with her in one fucking day?

Liache spots me walking across the street with no regard for the traffic, and waves me over. Her beautiful, dark hair is flitting in the light breeze that offers no respite from the incredible heat of the day. The warmth radiating from the pavement makes me feel like my feet are sinking into tar as I walk, and I try my hardest to walk like a normal human being.

I sit in an empty chair on an unoccupied side of the small square table, looking at Gabriel pointedly as his head swirls around my vision. "Good to see you again," I say with just the slightest hint of sarcasm.

Gabriel looks back at me in an almost challenging way in his confusion. I refuse to break eye contact through my sunglasses' dark, reflective lenses.

Liache breaks the awkward silence. "How was the interview?"

I shrug. At this point, I honestly can't remember how it went; I'm far too involved with staying in one place while the world tilts and spins, trying to knock me down. During a particularly nauseating whirl, I excuse myself, somehow managing to walk my way through the cafe doors and into their public restroom. My muscles contract violently and painfully as I dry heave for a few minutes above one of the toilets until my body produces some bile. There's not a lot in my system for it to reject right now. I pop a mint in my mouth and splash some cold water on my face, drying it with a paper towel before walking out as though everything was perfectly in order.

I order a coffee at the counter and take my place back at the table with Liache and that giant, walking phallus. I know what he's doing, and I'm helpless to fight back against it. I can see her slipping away from me, and I can't pull my head out of my ass long enough to stop it. Why am I like this?

"Are you alright?" Gabriel's voice rings, lashing against my eardrums and pulling me out of my musings.

"He's fucked up." Liache doesn't hesitate, nor does she look specifically pleased with this fact. Instead, she seems irritated.

Gabriel rolls his eyes and takes a sip from his fruity semen latte. There's bound to be fallout from this. The last time I went on a bender, he punched me in the face.

"Well, I can't wait to see this interview," he says, cracking a smile. He knows that, at the very least if I fucked it up it will get us some more media attention, which is never a bad thing. That's how we got this far in the first place.

I run my fingers through my hair, pushing back and away from my face as I struggle to concentrate on reality. I hate being in public. I hate people and I hate feeling like I must adhere to a social standard. I want very much to go home and remind Liache why she's with me, but I'll stick it out. She isn't exactly pleased with me, and I'll do whatever I can to make her happy.

Liache laughs a little bit Gabriel managed to lighten the mood. "Yeah, at the very least, it will be entertaining."

I know I thought I did a lot better than I actually did. I heave a deep sigh and take a drink of my own coffee, the bitterness of it cutting through the desert of my mouth like black, flavorful, life-giving rain. I realize that I really need to be drinking water right now, but decide I'll get to that later. Right now, I need the caffeine to clear my senses as much as it can.

It took a while this time, but the fairies are back. I do my best to ignore them but mindlessly swat one or two away from the edges of my vision before I finally turn my gaze to my breathtakingly gorgeous Liache.

"When's the next interview?" I ask, trying to sound like I'm being responsible, but everyone here knows that I'll forget and need to be carted in and sobered up for it. If there's even time. It's a lot more likely that it'll happen exactly like today.

"Two days," Liache responds, taking another sip of her own coffee. She knows better than to give me weekdays as an answer to that question, I would flounder hopelessly afterward.

I nod, acknowledging her answer, and toss back about half of my still-scalding coffee.

A loud, abrasive pinging sound pierces the relative silence, causing me to nearly jump out of my chair and Gabriel starts laughing. Normally, he's a rather stoic person, but right now, he's just taking great joy in watching me not enjoy my high. He pulls his phone out to check the notification. Turns out, it's a message from Luc with a link to an article already written about my interview today. There's a picture of me, looking like a deer caught in headlights, my pupils dilated beyond any logically sober point, shielding myself from the swarm of people trying to prepare me for being on camera.

Well, that's not how I remember it.

"Is that what your pupils look like?" Gabriel asks, snatching my sunglasses off my face, far too quickly for my impaired reflexes to prevent.

Sunlight immediately assaults my eyes, blinding me with its white-hot light and causing me to grunt in pain. I grope blindly for the glasses that Gabriel has in his hands as he cackles in sadistic amusement. I can hear Liache giggling along with him.

Well, at least she's happy.

I've opened myself up to this, and I know that. It still makes it seriously fucking annoying considering the fact that I'm positive Gabriel wants to bed what's mine.

He hands me back the sunglasses, offering sweet, sweet relief from the constant assault of fiery light. The searing pain in my temples, however, does not subside. Nature is too damn bright.

Eventually, what little conversation there was between Gabriel and Liache peters out, they grow tired of making fun of me and Liache and I head home.

The sun is setting, the air cooling off ever so slightly, and my drugs are starting to wear off. It's a relief right now, so that I can deal with Liache a little bit more soberly. The trees whipping past my window are a welcome grounding force for me, the few stars that are already visible are threatening to tear me back out into hallucinations.

Liache walks into the house ahead of me. I keep just enough distance between us for me to look at her glorious butt. I take the time to drink her in, the flowing mane of dark brown hair, the way that her clothes compliment her wonderful curves.

I hear the satisfying 'click' of the door latching behind me and feel the vibrations of the mechanisms in the lock grinding as I turn it. I realize suddenly that I'm not nearly as grounded as I thought I was.

Regardless, I wrap my hands around the warm, soft flesh of Liache's shoulders, smiling gently at her for just a moment before I slam her into the nearest wall and kiss her forcefully.

Her look of moderate annoyance with me is replaced at once by one of complete and utter desire. She kisses me back passionately, little squeaks and quiet moans escaping her as she pushes back against me.

I pick her up and carry her up the stairs, throwing her off me and watching her bounce as she lands on our bed. At this point, I begin seeing the faint outlines of the wings I'm positive she has, other people just can't see them. But sometimes I can, and that's how I know she's mine. She was made for me, and I need to do better for her.

She gasps as I climb on top of her, pinning her hands

down above her head and giving her exactly what she wants. She is exquisite, she is wonderful, she is more beautiful than anybody else in the world and she is mine.

I feel as though I'm being absorbed by her, breathing in her intoxicating, dark, and earthy scent as I kiss her again. I never want this to end.

I can see the colorful ribbon of curses and swears escaping her delicate lips as she utters them in complete ecstasy, I can feel the blistering scratches as her nails drag across the skin of my back. She forces me onto my back and takes control. Her wings are clearer now, more pronounced in their iridescence as they spread, spanning the width of our king-sized bed.

I grab hold of her hips as I close my eyes, and I feel like my entire body is slipping inside her as we both clearly reach the same, exquisite release. I can see inside her, I can easily see the anatomy of what's just happened, the different parts of her reproductive system as I hear hysterical laughter from somewhere not far off. I realize, abruptly, that it is the individual strands of DNA inside her eggs. I can see them twisting and untwisting and writhing in hysterics as they laugh at me.

I gasp and open my eyes as Liache collapses on top of me. I can feel her heart racing through her chest and that brings me out of my hallucinations. I hold her close as she catches her breath, her heat contributing to my own, our skin sticky with the same sweat. I kiss the side of her head gently before she gets up. She throws on some paint-covered clothes and then sits at the edge of the bed, smiling at me.

I want to tell her that I love her, but no matter how hard I try, the words just won't come out of my mouth. It's better that way. My love is toxic, it is destructive, painful, corrosive, and evil. So instead, I just smile gently back at her.

She squeezes my hand. "I have a commission I need to get done," she explains as she gets up and walks towards her in-home studio.

I don't argue, I don't say anything, I just get up to go shower. The water hitting my skin and beading off is mesmerizing, the sensation of warmth rolling off my back threatens to absorb me completely. Eventually, I manage to rinse the soap and shampoo off.

I get dressed in some dark, but comfortable clothes. My phone, which has been on its charger all day, begins to ring. It's Luc.

"Hey man, you gotta get over here," he says, hurriedly. "I have a present for you."

Luc often says things like this, it's a little bit confusing for me but I almost always oblige. Sometimes I think it's his way of dealing with the fact that his brother has a serious girlfriend, and I never really stop to think about what the implications of him calling me like I'm his single buddy are. I tell him I'll be there as soon as I can.

I walk slowly down the stairs, very sober now that it's been most of a day and I've had my shower. My wet hair is still clinging to my forehead.

"Liache," I call her name affectionately as I enter her little studio. Paint stains the layers upon layers of newspaper that she uses instead of a carpet rustling beneath her feet as she walks over to greet me. "Luc just called; he wants me to go over."

I know she'll show me the piece when it's done, but she never wants anybody to look at it until that point.

"Okay," she says, giving me a kiss but being careful not to touch me. It's been maybe an hour and she's covered in paint.

She doesn't seem displeased with me going to Luc's, she just takes the information as it's given and goes about her work. I guess it's kind of a good thing I'm leaving. When I'm home to bother her, it takes her forever to finish a piece. This way, I can do whatever with Luc and she can get the commission done.

The sketches on her wall from earlier today look suspiciously like a very nude Gabriel, but I file that away for later as well. He had absolutely been at her studio, I'm positive of it. Son of a bitch is infiltrating her life to get closer to her, I know it.

I take the short drive over to Luc's house in a car that is stuffy and warm, having not cooled down after the sun had set. Everything seems so dull; the colors of the world, my senses, the sounds of life whipping past me at what feels like 20 miles an hour.

I walk into Luc's house without knocking and am attacked

with a hug from the five-foot-nothing guitarist. The younger of the two brothers, if only by barely a year or two, is Luc, and he is, therefore, the more enthusiastic and ready to party of them.

The force from his hug sends us both onto the floor, me hitting first and then getting slammed with the weight of his body into my side. I let out a grunt of pain and then begin laughing when I see his gigantic grin.

He holds up two baggies that are full of cocaine. And then, he points at the table, where the hallucinogens are hiding.

"Presents!" he yells, his round face beaming with the glee of a small child on Christmas morning whose tree is positively buried in large boxes that are colorfully wrapped.

He gets up off the floor, offering me a hand up. I take it, and we set to work setting up our party zone for the night. Luc being Luc, he also has a fully stocked bar in the living room, and after helping him set out the drugs we'll be doing tonight, I go and get us each a few fingers of Scotch.

The more fucked up, the merrier, right?

Luc has some crazy, bullshit, pulsating music playing in the background, and in what seems like a few minutes, half of the cocaine is gone. We're both sitting at the edge of the couch and discussing hypothetical situations loudly with one another. What's going to happen when we're on tour, how excited he is about it because he loves it so much. And at this point, I can't help but to ask a question.

"Luc, tell me honestly," I say, begging him in earnest to speak the truth. "Do you think Gabriel wants to fuck Liache?"

He lets loose with a hyperactive giggle, breathing in and out a few times quickly to regain control of himself. "Dude, bro," he says, a huge smile still beaming at me. "Of course, he wants to fuck Liache. But, like, who doesn't? Have you seen Liache? The question you really want to ask is, do I think he could fuck Liache."

I pause for a moment that feels like forever before rephrasing my question. "Do you think he could?"

"I don't think he would, my friend." He pauses here to do another line, then exhales loudly through his mouth. "Not in a million years do I think he would. It's weird though, cause he's such a physically large guy like he's just huge, he's like the hulk, but he acts like this tiny, shy little boy. I mean unless he's busy punching you in the face." He looks at me with a thoughtful expression for a second, then rescinds his answer. "He wouldn't as long as you are in the picture. He'd hate himself for it."

I reposition myself slightly, turning to face Luc head-on as my heart jumps into my throat and begins beating rapidly. "Do you think she would?"

Luc begins to laugh again, this time much louder and heartier than before. He genuinely thinks this is hilarious. "Dude, she drank your fuckin' Kool-Aid," he says, plainly. "I have watched you do some shitty things to her, and she's still by your side. She is absolutely, one hundred percent, without the shadow of a doubt yours. She will watch you kill yourself and then happily clean up the shit from your drug-saturated corpse."

I laugh a little bit, sitting back and relaxing against the couch for a second before realizing that I have far too much energy for that. We need something to do, something active and fun. I sit forward again, the tension and restlessness in my muscles having risen to points beyond that of relaxation. What Luc said made me feel better, but now I'm just generally on edge. It shouldn't have made me feel better. I'm an asshole to her and everyone can see it. Nothing related to that should bring me comfort.

I've decided it's time for my favorite drug. I lean forward and place an indiscriminate amount of acid on my tongue.

"Luc, are you upset that your brother got a girl?" I ask quietly.

He sighs heavily, following suit with the acid. "I'm happy 'e's happy, you know?" he answers, there's a but coming, though. "*Tres jolie*, but there's a loneliness in it. He's my brother, he's been my best friend since I was born, it's weird to do shit without him." He sighs here.

It's strange, I realize I often don't believe that their native tongue is French, they've been here for so long, their accents are nearly undetectable. But right now, now that Luc and I are both so fucked up, he's having a harder time masking it. It's not how it is in the movies for them, though. There's no throaty, consonant-heavy accent, but more the occasionally missing 'h', a word or two that they once in a while forget the English word for.

"Where the fuck are you guys from?" I ask, without a hint of remorse for the phrasing.

"Quebec."

"Huh," I sit back in my seat, trying to think of what I know about that place. The answer to that is nothing. All I know is that it's in Canada and that they're not that sexy, European kind of French. I laugh a little to myself as I light a cigarette and inhale deeply.

My high has changed. This is no longer the hyper 'up' of our previous drug, and it's not the hazy hallucinogen that I'm used to, but an anxiety-inducing blend of the two that I'm not entirely comfortable with. In my eyes, the room gets darker despite the rising sun behind the curtains.

A slow, steady beat of whatever music Luc has playing now floats effortlessly to my eardrums, vibrating my entire body and lifting me with the tune. It feels like when a cartoon character smells something delicious and the scent carries them toward it, only more passionate. I close my eyes so I can concentrate on the changing sounds and block out any hallucinations. That, of course, doesn't work.

The intricate lines of the veins and capillaries inside of my eyelids are illuminated by the light of the rising sun, then twisting and turning and morphing into labyrinthine patterns before my mind starts to wander and my imagination superimposes images over the ever-changing backdrop. At first, I just see Liache in all her beauty, her ethereal wings exposed for only me to see, and then she backs away from me, still smiling and dancing in the sunshine. The heroic figure of a shadowy man joins her, sporting wings of his own. After a few moments, I recognize him as Gabriel, and he starts to kiss her. I gasp, open my eyes and sit up abruptly, making Luc jump in surprise.

"None of that," he manages to squeak through nervous laughter.

I look at him, studying his morphing face as I see that his pupils have completely overtaken the sclera of his eyes. It's a terrifying sight, and it takes me a minute to remember that I've taken some drugs and should not be trusting my own eyes.

We both start laughing hysterically. I have no idea how long we are in this state, but it feels like seconds later that we're walking up the footpaths between his home and mine. There are a lot of different, branching paths, and this is seriously ill-advised, but here we are anyway. The crunch of the gravel beneath our feet is oddly satisfying but leaves me trying desperately to tiptoe around this forest in the dead of night.

How long have we been out here?

I have an earth-shaking epiphany; I don't care how long we've been out here. I don't care if we find our way to my house before the next day, and I don't particularly care about any upcoming interviews I have. I like the rush I get from being on the stage, I love the incomprehensible roar of the crowd, I love singing. I don't love all the bullshit that comes along with it.

I shake my head and look behind me, making sure I haven't lost Luc. He gives me the thumbs up and begins to laugh again. When I turn back around to look where I'm going, I trip on a fallen branch and land flat on my face.

Luc is in hysterics. At this point, he is laughing so hard he can barely breathe, and that makes me laugh, too. From the corner of my blurred vision, I can see him trying to approach me while doubled over, bleating laughter emanating from his gaping mouth. Not exactly his most flattering of moments, but then again, it isn't mine, either.

The thought crosses my mind that as much as I love having him here, this is not what I'm used to. I'm used to being alone, solitary in my hallucinations and my musings, my self-hatred, but having Luc here has kept me from that latter aspect of my journeys.

He offers his hand to help me up, still laughing. I take it, stand and try to get my bearings. Near, I can see the pond I most often find myself sitting at during my lonely trips. I walk over to it and squat down at the water's edge, squeezing my knees to my chest with one arm and creating ripples with my other hand.

The light reflecting off the surface of the water is broken with each tiny wave, fracturing the image of the moon and stars and morphing it into something terrifying. Once more, this image takes the dark and ghastly form of some kind of monster, a demon, and I take off running in the direction of the house.

Luc struggles to keep up behind me, yelling for me to slow down so he can catch up, and without my noticing, without any inkling of how I ended up here, I am flat on my back on the ground, pain radiating from the back of my head and shoulders. I open my eyes, sucking the cool air in between my teeth in a painful hiss.

Fuck.

Above me stands Liache, Gabriel, and Marc, and not one of them looks happy to see either of us. I hear Luc skid to a stop somewhere above my head, sending pebbles flying onto my face. My best approximation of the situation is that in my blind terror, Gabriel managed to clothesline me.

Now it is Gabriel who offers his hand to help me up, a grim and austere look gracing his shockingly chiseled features. As he lifts my weight with incredible ease, I can't help but to compare myself to him. I am thin and weak, my features seem exaggerated on a sunken face, worsened by the dark tone of my shoulder-length hair. Gabriel has long, slender facial features, a strong chin, and wavy, chin-length chestnut hair. The cherry on top of his robust powerhouse of a body. At this moment, I know they are fucking. And if they haven't yet, then they will.

They're of the same marble. They are beautiful and glowing and absolutely belong together. But I can't let her go. I narrow my eyes at Gabriel before walking away, into the house, where I'm sure both Luc and I are about to be lectured by our impromptu family.

I sit on the couch, almost missing it, and then righting myself in the seat as Luc sits beside me, looking like a scolded puppy.

Light begins to flood the room, leaking in through the windows as the sun rises on the third day of our bender, and I know exactly why everyone looks so furious. We lost two full days in the middle of doing promotions.

Gabriel stands back, arms crossed over his massive chest, looking like an angry bodyguard as Liache lays into me.

"Where the hell were you two?" her voice is a high-pitched mess of anger right now, pealing against my eardrums and threatening to do serious damage. I flinch visibly as she continues. "We went to Luc's house. The back door was wide fucking open, and both of your phones were sitting on the table next to a pile of drugs that was clearly a lot bigger before you got to it." Liache starts to pace as she speaks, now slightly calmer and sounding almost relieved, but still clearly irate. "I called the hospitals, I called the police, but they wouldn't file a report, and this is fucking why!" She stops pacing and screams this last part at us, her face contorting in rage, and tears begin to pour from her eyes.

The world around her is morphing, but she is perfectly clear, her wings are perfectly clear and so are Gabriel's. Marc is standing next to Gabriel, all worry, no anger. He just wanted his little brother back.

I can feel the chemicals trickling down from the top of my head through the rest of my body as Liache begins to cry. Running through my veins now is pure anxiety. There is a sinking feeling in my chest as the high stops abruptly and absolutely and I stand to wrap my arms around her warm, shivering figure.

It doesn't last long. She shoves me back down onto the couch and slaps me across the face. The sound and the sensation hit me at the exact same time, though I do not see it coming.

The slap echoes through the house, hanging in the air as though time had stopped. Dead silence descends on the room. It is thick and unbreakable, and nobody has any idea what to do. I just sit on the couch, a wounded man, knowing I've done wrong and not knowing how to fix it. Luc still sits on the couch next to me, unsure of his own next actions.

It doesn't matter anyway. The biggest conflict here is between me and Liache, and Gabriel, for some weird reason.

I'm totally convinced that they're sleeping together at this point.

There's a moment where Luc goes to hug his brother, apologizing profusely for disappearing like that. It'll never happen again, he says.

Well, that's not true, and he and I both know it, but that's really between the two of us.

Right now, I'm busy hating myself for upsetting Liache as much as I have. She's never slapped me before, even through all of my previous benders, and my going missing for days on end, and all of the bullshit that I've put her through, she's never, not once, slapped me for any of it.

She must really be angry now.

Luc and Marc leave, doubtlessly to go clean up the pile of drugs still left on his coffee table from when we were busy snorting it. And that's fine. It was a good time and he and I bonded quite a bit. The problem is, that Gabriel doesn't leave. He stands by Liache's side as she continues being angry at me. Neither of them is saying anything, and that's really upsetting for me. I don't particularly like where this has been going. Within the span of three days, I've seen them together three times, twice on the same day, and Lord knows how long he's been here since I've been gone. Yet I continue to stare at him as though I'm challenging him to a contest. I dare him to lay hands on my woman.

It's too late for my psyche though, I'm already convinced they've been together, I just don't know how long. Nor do I care. She's still mine, and I'm determined to show that. Not right now, but eventually I'll have another chance at it.

I think about how much pain I must have caused her in the past few days, and I hate myself a little bit more for each second that I consider it. I'm horrible, I am evil, and I am a pain, and I can't believe she loves me, but she seems to. She keeps choosing my stringy ass over his, and for that, I am eternally grateful.

I pull myself out of my musings for a moment to ask them an imperative question.

"What the fuck is going on between you two?" I ask, still positive that this had happened, that they had happened.

Both offer me a look of complete and utter confusion. I am mistaken. There is a very real possibility that the drugs have led me to believe something happened that hadn't yet happened.

"Is that really what this is about?" Liache asks in earnest. "Do you really think that after all this time, all that the three of us have been through together, that either of us would do that to you?" She sighs and looks at me with pure disdain. "I don't even know where you got the idea. Nothing has changed."

I look at Gabriel, who still looks confused as a toddler having calculus explained to them. He seems very much at a loss for words.

"Sure," I mutter under my breath, obviously I don't believe them.

I'll take it for now. But I know what he's doing, I know where this is going and I'm helpless to stop it. At least for now. I'll find a way. She was made for me, there's no way that he'll take her from me. Not ever. I'll make sure of it.

Liache walks Gabriel to the door, insisting that he can leave, that he should leave, she and I need to talk. He asks if she's sure and she nods, acting like I can't hear them. But I can.

Before Gabriel even leaves, I'm already lying in our bed, waiting to fall asleep whether Liache is with me or not. It doesn't matter to me anymore. Right now, I am furious, and I just want to forget that today ever happened. Oddly enough, I'm not even interested in having sex with Liache, which is a constant goal for me. I just want to go to sleep.

After just a few hours of sleep, I drive myself to the radio interview I have today. Marc has sent me a text with the location and time, and I'm determined to prove that I'm an adult and I can take care of shit on my own, without Gabriel or Liache breathing down my neck.

I feel like they're my parents right now rather than my lover and my friend. Gabriel feels farther from being my friend than he ever has and that's upsetting to me. If there's ever anyone I can count on to keep me on my feet, it's him.

Regardless, I waltz into my interview, high again after having done more drugs on my way in. I have decided, officially, that I don't like being with people when I'm high, I much prefer being on my own. The radio guy introduces himself to me and I just blink at him. There's no real need to introduce myself and he chuckles back at me nervously. I refuse to take off my sunglasses.

The interview is going about as well as can be expected. He asks questions about the tour, I have answers this time. He asks what it's like being so easily recognizable when I'm out trying to live my life, and I tell him he'd be surprised at how few people actually fucking recognize you.

Of course, we're live on the air so the radio personality guy is having a difficult time censoring me, which is fine, I don't give a shit. This is me and often, this is how my interviews go. Only this one gets a little bit too personal, through no fault of Mr. DJ-face.

He asks me an innocent enough question, "What is it like being on the road when you have a family at home?"

My answer is irate and there is no hesitation whatsoever. "I don't have a family. I have a girlfriend who refuses to go on tour with me. Not because there's anything particularly important happening here at home, but because there's a ridiculous love triangle happening and I'm fucking helpless to stop it. My drummer is an asshole, but I still consider him one of my closest friends. My family is my band, and when we're on the road, everything is perfect, I can forget about the shit that I go through here without any remorse. The screaming fans are my family, the road is my family."

The radio guy looks mortified. At some point, he's cut to commercial, but I'm not sure when. I regret the very public meltdown as soon as the words have escaped my lips but leave after apologizing to the host. It's not his fault, shit, I'm the one who's a total fucking mess.

I drive home and once again, somehow make it back alive.

Within minutes, an entire bottle of whiskey is gone and I'm sure I'm about to be scolded by Liache.

When she comes back, obviously having heard the interview, she doesn't actually seem to care. She tells me that our ticket sales spiked and that our manager has seen fit to add a few dates on to the beginning of the tour. She doesn't care, she seems all sunshine and roses like she normally does. I wonder what has happened to make her so complacent in our relationship. I dismiss the thought and busy myself with teasing her while she works on cleaning up the kitchen I haven't eaten in since what seems like months ago.

I poke at her side repeatedly until she turns to look at me, her face puckered and contorted in frustration.

This is the moment she finally snaps.

"So let me get this straight," her voice cracks like a whip, loud and brisk. "You manage to convince yourself that I'm sleeping with Gabriel, and then you straight up disappear for two days hoping to accomplish what exactly?" She sighs and leans back against the counter she had just been wiping down.

I don't have an answer for her, I just continue my clueless and consistent stare into her eyes while the whole world morphs around her. Several minutes of silence pass between us before she says anything further.

"I don't like this," her voice is quiet now, scared. She's nearly whispering, her voice ringing out into our silent house like a prayer. "I don't like you like this. We've been together for so long now, we've built a life together, we love each other, what changed?"

Another question I can't answer. It dawns on me that this is in my head. Gabriel hasn't been flirting with her, at least, not any more than he ever had. We've always been close. Even before Marc and Luc, it had always been us. And now, I'm pushing them both away.

"Why am I like this?" the sound of my own voice in my throat surprises me. It was as though it had involuntarily leaked out, radiating from my chest and forming words that I wasn't aware were in my head, but they are. I slide down the wall I'm leaning against, sitting on the floor and extending my legs in front of me. "I'm sorry."

Liache comes to me and sits beside me, the world begins to melt away from us and we are sitting on the only stable part of existence. Nothing else in the world matters but her. My entire existence is about her and always has been about her and I need to keep it that way.

I need to worship her the way she deserves to be worshiped.

There are stars on our morphing ceiling, and everything looks like it's melting away in huge dollops of oil paint. Except for her. She shields me from this incessant rain of creativity with her iridescent wings. I am so blessed. I marvel at her angelic beauty as she leans toward me.

I feel the soft suppleness of her full lips against my own, the earthy smell of her perfume intoxicates me, infecting my senses and demanding a full, complete, and utter surrender from me. Before I know it, I am naked and on the floor with Liache, the only thing shielding us from the painted world are her shining wings.

This isn't about desire, this isn't about the finish or control or even personal pleasure, this is about exploring each other. Time seems to have slowed as my hands wander her entire body, my lips taste her delicate mouth as I worship her body.

This is our apology. It is slow, sweet, and beautiful. The softness of her skin lights fire to my senses, the skirting of her lips against my neck drives me to near insanity, and I wouldn't have it any other way. The delicate moments in our lives, the ones that seem to last forever, those are the ones we need to cherish, and I plan to cherish this for eternity.

At some point, she gasps, and two breathy, desperate words appear from her mouth and float in the air on the ribbon of utterances spilling forth; "Don't stop."

In this moment, I am a slave to her. Anything she wants, anything at all, I will give to her.

The sound of her desperate moans reverberates against the barriers of silence in the rest of our home, threatening to tear the delicate fiber of our existence. I can almost see the laws of physics fighting against the very idea as her groans taper off in satisfaction.

She's laying with her head on my chest, listening as my heartbeat slows to its normal rate. The feeling of her softness in my arms is what I live for, what I'd die for.

"You're my angel," I whisper gently.

"I know. I love you."

"I know." I still can't say it. The words are there, begging me to be released into the ether, and I can't bring myself to do it. I can't let myself love her; I will destroy her if I do.

I don't know how long we stay on the checkered floor of our kitchen, but it is at least until the house begins to reconstruct itself. Slowly but surely, the paint dripping from every surface begins to slow, and eventually stop, though everything still looks slightly bulbous, as though the paint had simply dried instead of ceasing to exist. It's a beautiful, however unsettling effect.

We both get up, and Liache puts her clothes back on before returning to her earlier task. I walk back up to our room without bothering, carrying my clothes in my hand. I drop them with the rest of the laundry and put on something more comfortable before fishing more drugs out of my drawer stash.

She may have put my suspicions to bed, but not my issues.

I slip the drugs into my mouth and the world tilts in a very unsettling and disjointed way. Everything goes black and I feel my head hit the floor without any pain. I can hear Liache's hurried footsteps as she rushes to see what happened, and then, silence.

2

I am in and out of consciousness for God knows how long. I vaguely remember Marc inducing vomiting while Gabriel supported my weight, and Luc trying to talk to me while Liache whimpered in the corner of the room. I don't remember what order it happened in, nor if any of it is real, but it's awfully specific to have been fabricated.

For a few hazy moments, I can see Luc sitting at the side of my bed, his eyebrows knitted in concern, his hands clasped tightly under his chin. I open my eyes fully and see Marc standing behind him, the same round face sporting the same concerned expression before I smile at them and slip back into whatever trance this is.

The next time I gain any modicum of consciousness, I see Gabriel. Somehow, I know he hasn't left. His eyes are red, I can see the tears in his eyes threatening to fall, and I laugh a little bit. He cracks a smile and flips me off.

"Hey, fuck you," My voice crackles through split lips from a parched throat.

I think about how once, he and I were the same. We were small and lanky, with no muscle mass and no hope at all with girls. Once upon a time, we were the same kid in the same high school facing the same bullshit acne problems and suddenly, I can't believe the way I have been thinking about him. I can't believe the way I have been treating Liache and I certainly can't believe that at one point, I thought he didn't give a shit about me beyond the band.

I try to sit up and Liache puts another pillow behind me. She offers me some water and I realize that we are absolutely in my room. I am slightly surprised that we're not at a hospital.

A lump rises in my throat and I try my hardest to battle it back, but I can't.

"Gabriel," I utter his name before clearing my throat, also struggling to beat back tears that have already escaped my eyes. "I'm so fucking sorry. I know you would never do that to me. I know... I'm sorry."

There's nothing else that I can say. Nothing at all. It's obvious that he has nothing else to communicate, but I know he's the only one who didn't leave my side today. I know that even Liache had to walk away and clear her head, but not him.

"Stop doing this shit to yourself, seriously," he says, voice cracking ever so slightly. He looks over at the door, where Liache just disappeared, and then back at me. "She deserves better, and so do you."

A few moments later, Luc comes bounding up the stairs like a golden retriever puppy excited to see his human, then belly flops onto the bed next to me.

"You're awake!" he exclaims, obviously overjoyed at this development. "Thank God, man. I was really worried about you for a while there."

Marc had left once he figured out I would live. That's fine by me. He never was one to stick around in heavy situations.

Liache approaches my side and kisses my forehead from beside the bed, next to where Gabriel is seated. I look up at her exhausted face, see where the mascara has stained her cheeks, where the tears had run, and I realize how much pain I have put her through.

As a result of the crash from the drugs more than anything else (or at least that's what I tell myself), I begin to cry. My chest heaves as I struggle to get oxygen and tears stream down my face. Liache hugs me as the boys pat my back, and oddly enough, I'm comforted.

I know that while I want to change, I want to be better for her, for them, for me, it won't last long. I know that while I love the idea of getting off drugs and being better for Liache, even becoming a father, it won't happen long-term.

The drugs are my soul mate, and I am powerless against them.

My best guess of what happened is that it wasn't the drugs that got me this time. It was the huge bottle of whiskey that I downed with abandon. Either way, within a couple of days, I'm completely recovered, though going a little lighter on the controlled substances than I would normally.

It's a good thing.

At some point, I've watched the television interview that I

did, and it went a lot more poorly than I remember it going. I'm articulate as always in the actual interview, but it's clear how dilated my pupils are, and on my exit, I took down the whole lighting system and a camera before just walking out the door as though nothing happened.

It's completely taken over the internet.

Once more, the ticket sales for the tour have gone up, which is unsurprising. People love a train wreck, and they want a chance to see me wreck the train on the stage. Voyeurs, the lot of them.

The radio interview has also ended up online, with several million hits. Let it never be said that my bad habits aren't good for business, because they are. They are phenomenal for business.

Marc, Luc, and Gabriel are enjoying every second of this, just like the rest of the world, and I find this comforting.

I very nearly destroyed myself, and them in the process, and yet they can find humor in it, they can laugh at my shortcomings more than the potential downfall of us.

They really do feel like family.

We've finally gotten a night of practice in between all of the interviews and making sure the bus is ready to go, my issues and recovery, and it is glorious.

This is my favorite part of my art.

This is the part where the emotion takes you away. Fear and anger and love and hate and happiness all well within you as the instruments blare over the amps, and the amps shake the world. You can feel the beat of the music, and it is part of your soul. It is divine, beautiful, and perfect, and it is God's gift to me.

My voice rings forth from my chest, weakening my knees, my arms, my entire body as pure heart bleeds from my mouth. Silence is my canvas, the wavelengths are my paint, and what is created is always perfection. There are no wrong answers.

The ringing tinnitus of silence lapses for just a few seconds before Gabriel leads in with a slow, sluggish, and steady beat. Luc picks up with a sad melody and at the same time, Marc compliments that melody, harmonizing with it perfectly. I let the sounds wash over me, taking over my body, feeling the emotion, feeling the pain, and the pleasure, everything they hope to inflict

This is important. This is release, this is love and hate and beauty and ugliness in their imperfect glory. This is what I do, what I was made for, or... is it how I cope with not doing what I was made for?

This is how I imagine heaven. Everything good, and everything terrible, ringing forth from within my body, and from without. Honesty and innocence in their purest forms.

This is how I cleanse my soul.

Marc needs to go; he's got a hot date and can't be assed to hang out with us anymore. It's fine, eventually, they'll get used to the groove and she'll spend some time with us.

Maybe.

Come to think of it, Marc didn't really spend much time with us in the first place. Oh well.

That is his loss.

Luc, Gabriel, and I spend a little more time playing little bullshit tunes, coming up with little ditties for stupid old limericks before we all head back to Gabriel's house.

I think his house is the most interesting out of all of ours. It seems the most lived in, with the most personality. His interests are plastered all over that house. Different percussion instruments line the walls, hiding in the corners of each room. There are interesting sculptures on the bookshelves, which are also jam-packed with literary classics. It has a distinct and pleasant smell, something earthy and spicy and so specific to him that nobody could ever hope to replicate it, and there is interesting artwork on the walls. Some Salvador Dali, some Van Gogh, and...

The last time I was here, I spotted something odd in the room, and this time, after some shots and other things with Luc, I wander around the house, following the walls and paying particular attention to the artwork. Quite a few of these are Liache's, works from the beginning of her taking commissions until now. Not every piece that she has done is here but there is a good number of them, including her latest one.

I don't know whether to confront him or to hold on to that information for now. Perhaps I've filed him in my head under 'do not fuck with', but I'm not sure. I kind of want to punch him in the face right now.

I return to the chair I've officially claimed and continue imbibing with Luc while Gabriel drums an upbeat tune on a set of bongos, I can only assume he bought originally as a novelty.

We all get comfortable, and I even forget about all the paintings on his walls that my girlfriend did for a few minutes, when Gabriel's phone rings. He answers and I can hear him assuring Liache that everything is fine, I'm alright and he would make sure I got home safe.

Why does that always happen?

I fish my own phone out of my pocket and turn on the screen, realizing that it's been on silent, and I've missed 15 calls.

And there it is again. The self-doubt I had just barely quashed, the suspicions that I had put to bed. And there goes life, proving me wrong for trusting him.

It's fine though, I'll bide my time with him. I trust Liache, and that's all that matters.

But do I? It crosses my mind suddenly that these suspicions, this nagging feeling that I have, my paranoia wouldn't be prevalent, it wouldn't be so consuming and persistent. Would it be that way if I wasn't on to something? Wouldn't I rest easier if I was so certain that I had nothing to fear? I spend what feels like forever going over and over this in my head. I'm confused, frustrated. I'm in overdrive, spiraling out.

"Hey," Luc's voice cuts through the chaos, a welcome distraction. "Are you alright?"

"Yeah," my voice is quiet, reserved. "Yeah, I'm fine. I think I'm done though; I need to get home."

Luc casts me a sideways glance. He knows that I'm never done, he knows that I'll party until I physically drop, but he also knows that after what happened, I've slowed down.

I bid Luc a good night, and Gabriel drives me home, being clearly the soberest person available. The ride goes by in relative silence, there is a small smattering of forced conversation as Gabriel drives from his home to mine, as though it's something he does every day.

We are nearly there when my restraint breaks. "Do you love her?"

"No." His response is short and sweet, but aloof and

cautious. It is not comforting in the least.

I work my hardest to not spiral out alone in the car with him, but it doesn't really work. I replay his singular word in my head, on an endless loop of analytical nonsense, assessing the tone, the clarity, the perceived intention. I obsess in the two minutes that seem like eternity remaining in the drive, get out of the car at my house, not saying a word to him. He knows me well enough to know I don't believe him, and he also knows that there's nothing he can do to make me.

Whatever, it's fine, I'll live.

When I walk into the house, Liache is in the shower. I walk directly into her studio and look at the study sketches on the wall from her art classes, paying particular attention to the sketches of Gabriel. They're clearly from the day I picked her up from that class when I saw them walking out together.

It wouldn't be so bad if it weren't a traditional art class, where they cart in one model or another and have them pose completely nude in front of the class. It wouldn't be so bad if it didn't seem as though the perspective Liache got in that class wasn't a head-on shot of his junk. It wouldn't be so bad if it didn't look like Gabriel had done that on purpose.

But it was, it did, and he had.

I was positive about all these things. The question was quickly becoming one of whether she enjoyed the view or not.

I walk out of her studio and into the kitchen, looking for anything to drink or take. I can't handle this level of suspicion; I need to knock myself out.

I find a bottle of vodka, take three shots, and go to bed.

Of course, by this time, Liache is just getting out of the shower. She walks over to the bed, not bothering to cover herself, and lays down beside me. I offer no reaction to her gentle caresses, instead just closing my eyes and trying my hardest to sleep.

This isn't a conversation we need to have anymore, it's a situation I need to prove.

I have decided it's high time to try being an actual friend to Marc once again. I am meeting up with him for a talk over a socially acceptable stimulant: coffee.

Once, we were close, we all were. Then at some point, Marc met this woman. And that's fine, like Luc, I'm happy for him, but I miss him being around once in a while outside of official business. It feels like pulling teeth to get him to come to the jam hall for practice, and there's no hope in getting him to come out partying with us after that, which is most of what we do.

I wonder if he's officially sober while I wait for him to arrive, having already ordered my coffee and chosen a table.

He finally shows up, not at all the person I remember him being. He's all fun and games when Luc is around but on his own, he's just boring.

Marc is pleasant enough with me, making small talk like a real adult for a few minutes before I just can't take it anymore. I hate small talk; I hate being in public and I certainly hate being sober.

"Hey, Marc," I start tenderly, not sure exactly how to go about breaching the topic of him saving my life. "Thank you for being there when I, uh, had my little issue."

"You mean the day when I literally stuck my fingers down your t'roat so that you wouldn't die?" he asks dismissively, like it was no big deal. "Don't mention it. Ever. I do not need to be reminded of that time I was covered from head to toe in your vomit." He cracks a slight grin and takes a sip of his coffee. "At least it was mostly whiskey."

I scoff, fiddling with the lid of my drink absentmindedly. We sit in silence for several minutes before I look up at him, dead in the eyes with a crooked smirk. I miss the friendship we once had. It was always him, Luc, Gabriel, and me, tearing it up and having a blast, playing our stupid games and our stupid music and just generally having fun.

"What happened, man?" The question just appears between us, and now I can't take it back. I'm not sure that I'm ready for the answer that he can doubtlessly supply. Regardless, I'm in for the ride and I might as well hear what he has to say. There are a lot of things I've been ignoring lately.

"You went off the deep end," there is little to no

hesitation between my question and his answer. It's a fair point, I'll take the criticism. "You just, you went too 'ard for too long, and you started doing drugs that I just 'ad no interest in and frankly, *mon ami*, I got fucking tired of watching you destroy yourself, and Liache by extension."

I've focused my gaze on the sugar packets on the table, poking them around pointedly as though it is way more important than what he's saying, but I'm hearing everything, absorbing it as though the information is vital to my survival, and it might well be.

"*Regarde*, I love you guys, but I 'ave something good going for me now, and I'm not going to let what you do ruin it for me. I am coming on this tour, and I know that we'll bond again, and we will 'ave fun and we will get fucked up together again, this does not change anything, but I am protecting what is good and right in my life, and I feel like you should take a step back and do the same."

I forgot how much thicker his accent was than Luc's, how much harder of a time he had remembering the English words for random shit. I got the gist of it though; I know what he's saying and I'm going to try my hardest to take it to heart.

"Thank you, Marc."

"I would not 'ave saved your life if I did not consider you a good friend, *grand loup*," he laughs slightly as he stands up to walk away. "But you do need to work on not devouring little girls."

He raps gently on the table twice and walks away, leaving me to marinate in the wake of all he had said to me. I thought he was being distant, I thought that he hated me or that something in him had fundamentally changed, but that wasn't the case. He was avoiding me because I am toxic, and honestly, I was happy for that. The people who get close to me are the ones most likely to get hurt.

Maybe he's right. Maybe I have gone off the deep end, maybe I do need to work on bettering myself, but I don't even know where to begin. How do you start when your issues are such a huge and fundamental part of who you are? Confusion sets in, twisting my brain within its claws, threatening to devour my sanity. How do I start? Where does it end? How much of me is drugs and how much of me is me? What if I stop and there's nothing left?

I decide that I do need to cut back, legitimately, intentionally, and not because of a near-death experience. Liache deserves that much, the boys deserve that much. And who knows? I might find a reason to stick around.

The average life expectancy of someone in my position, with my habits and lifestyle, is 27. I've already nearly undercut that by two. I need to slow down, spend some time with Liache, learn how to be a functional person.

I stand up from the table, realizing that in my rumination, I've opened the packets of sugar and arranged the grains in lines, the way I would with any other drug. I laugh a little to myself and walk out, intent, for once, on being sober for the day.

For once in my life, I'm not focusing on what could go wrong, what inevitably will go wrong, I'm not focusing on whether or not Gabriel and Liache are conspiring against me behind my back, I'm not focusing on the negative. Everything is a little bit brighter, a little bit happier. For once, I'm okay.

Maybe I'm not doomed, after all. Maybe I've truly been given a divine gift, a chance to repent and redeem myself. What if this existence isn't the punishment, I had already decided it was?

I walk into the house, and Liache is at her art class. Or her writing group, I can't remember which, and I actually set to work cooking dinner for the two of us. Something I used to do and haven't in a long time.

I'm going to stay sober and have a lovely evening with my girlfriend.

It's been a while since that day, and things have been good. Actually good. Liache and I have been on a few double dates with Marc and Ann, I have not been doing as many drugs, things are looking up once again, as they so rarely do. It's been a while since I sabotaged myself, it's been a while since I felt like I needed hallucinogens to deal with real life. Things are better this way, Liache is happy, the music is getting practiced, the interviews are going better, more cleanly. I'm careful though, incredibly careful, to avoid the topic of how much better I've been doing. Ticket prices continue to go up while people still think I'm about to completely lose my mind.

I've even been to a doctor and discussed all of my problems, my paranoia, but definitely not my belief of Liache being an angel. That's my little secret. They put me on some pill or another, it makes it easier for me to decipher the insanity from what's actually happening. Though I still think that Gabriel went to her art class, and did it on purpose, I don't think she's in cahoots with him anymore. I don't think they're conspiring against me, and it's been better.

We are getting ready for dinner, the night before the boys and I leave for the tour. It's just something we've always done, congregated after everything was ready to go and drink and eat and make merry before we all leave. It was ritualistic and I think it was mostly for Liache. She doesn't like to be on the road, and I can respect that. She loves me, and she trusts me, and I trust her, and although she signed up to support me and has been a saint about all my issues, she didn't sign up to go on tour with us. And that's fair.

There are bags of clothing and stage gear piled up in a corner by the front door, things I'm going to need while I'm on the road. Months' worth of my medication, months' worth of baby powder, months' worth of throat lozenges, cough medicine, aloe gel. The stupid shit that vocalists ingest to make sure their vocal cords are in good condition, but nevermind my smoking, ignore all the warning labels on each pack, the fact that it causes irreparable harm to your mouth, throat, and lungs. The express reason I carry a cigarette case is, so I never have to look at those warnings. I can look at a picture of a naked woman instead.

It's just a lot more pleasant than warnings about that which could kill you.

Liache has finished putting on her face and has come back into our room, looking stunning, as always. Her short dress accentuates all the right places on her body, the red fabric peeking through the black lace overlay is delightfully flirty, her shoes put her at nearly my height. Her eyes are lined in charcoal smoke, the tint on her lips is that of a red rose. I want to ravish her where she stands. She is perfect, the picture of beauty.

"Liache," her name leaves my lips like a kiss blown on the wind. "You're so beautiful." I wrap my arms tightly around her tiny figure and kiss her forehead gently.

Every tour, it's the same restaurant, same time, same rushed, ecstatic, nostalgic feeling attached to the night. The excitement charges the air, leaves a trail behind every moment in the night, every time we do this.

We forget about the incredible complexities of our lives, the miracle that any of us sit here now, after struggling to get here, and breaking out onto the scene like fucking dynamite. With the amount of money our record label has upped us since my public meltdowns, it's surprising I haven't gone back off the deep end, it's surprising that so far all I've chosen to do is pay doctor's bills and go on medication to fix myself with it. Of all things.

I started my night drinking a nice, smoky-tasting whiskey, and within an hour, degenerated to doing shots of shitty tequila with Luc at the bar while Marc and Ann flirt disgustingly with one another, and Gabriel and Liache chat. She has spent most of the night chatting with him, much to my dismay.

I'm still convinced that he's an asshole, I'm still convinced that he wants her for his own, and I know damn well that that's what he's doing right now. It's fine. She's mine and I know it, I know I can trust her, but the way she's laughing, the intent in her eyes as she hangs off his every word is lighting a fire, I thought I'd long forgotten in my chest.

Something is off.

Luc doesn't really notice a change in my demeanor, and that's good. I don't want anybody to realize what's going through my head, what I want is for everybody to remain comfortable and continue on doing what they're doing so that I can marinate in it. So that I can soak it in and analyze and obsess.

I need to know what she's thinking, and what he thinks he's doing, and the best way for me to get in on that is to watch every single gesture. So that's exactly what I do. I watch as Liache barely touches her drink, as Gabriel talks and talks and talks, and she laughs and smiles and eventually becomes visibly tired. The entire time I'm obsessing and observing, Luc is trying and failing to flirt with girls at the bar.

I get distracted from surveilling my angel interact with that slab of beef we call a drummer when I hear a loud gasp and ice cubes hitting the floor abruptly. I look up at Luc's back seconds before he turns around, blinking and soaking wet.

"I did not count on *la chienne* knowing French," his voice is flat and unamused as he dries his face off with a napkin. "*Merde.*"

I can't help myself; I start laughing at him. My muscles ache as my body shakes with howling laughter. And I just can't stop. There's no reason I should be laughing at this length, it wasn't nearly that funny. I guess that the sudden break from my obsession combined with the punctuation of him saying something lewd to a woman in French and being understood is just too much for me, the shock is making me laugh harder than I should.

It is at this precise moment that I realize I'm shitfaced. The reason that I've come to this realization is actually really simple. It takes me a second, but I realize that my ass is no longer on a bar stool. My ass is no longer on anything; however, my face has met the floor with a sudden, numb 'thump'.

I laugh harder, Luc laughs harder. Soon, he and I are both sitting on the floor, laughing like idiots with our backs up against the bar. Marc comes over, offers his hand to both of us to get us to our feet. We both oblige, stand, and offer him a hug before he leaves. He's done for the night, and he's not looking particularly amused by our current shenanigans. That's fine, he'll be joining us after tomorrow, the way he always has. It's interesting to see though, the way he is around Ann compared to the way he used to be with us.

Gabriel is playing designated driver for us right now. Me and Luc are in the back seat of Gabriel's car, Liache is sitting shotgun, Gabriel looks concerned for her.

I'm still goofing off with Luc, we're poking around at each other, laughing, he'll say something in French that I can only assume is lewd, and I laugh harder, but I notice what's happening in that front seat.

It crosses my mind, during my roughhousing in the back

seat with my friend, that if I were a better man, I'd let him have her. He obviously loves her, and he does so in a way that I couldn't ever. I'm too selfish, I'm too destructive, I'm too evil. But this was my punishment, this is what God has given me, to live this life, loving somebody so wholly, so completely, and not being good enough to give her what she deserves. God has let me taste divine and pure love and made me unable to accept it.

Gabriel drops me and Liache off at our house, and I give Luc a hug as he gets into the front passenger seat before heading into the house with Liache.

She doesn't even take off her dress and kicks her shoes off lazily once she's already lying down on our bed, without getting under the blankets. I rub her back gently until she falls asleep, cover her with a smaller blanket from elsewhere in the house, and then head for my stash.

It's been a while since I bothered using, but tonight seems like as good a night as any. We're about to head out on tour, I'm already pleasantly intoxicated, the night is clear and warm, the forest is calling me as it always does.

I'm already outside when the drugs kick in, walking through the trees, chain smoking. I pull a slender cigarette from my case, the naked lady on the front winks as I snap it shut. I guffaw as I shove the case back into my back pocket. New cigarette in my mouth, I'm puffing to light it from the burning ember still smoking gently on the filter from the last one. I succeed, stomping the discarded filter and looking around as the fairies I haven't seen in so long come out to play. They float and flutter, cheerfully flying between the trunks and leaves of trees, teasing one another and occasionally diving at my head. I duck instinctively and once again, end up on my face on the ground. The dirt is dry and gritty here against my sweaty cheek. I dust my face off and look toward the sky, on my back now.

I ruminate in the moonlight, thinking about all that I know to be true. I'm amazed that we've come this far, me and the boys, that I've been allowed to poison and infect the masses with messages, but then again, I always knew I'd be well-received.

There are voices in my head again, rambling overlapping nonsense, things I can't quite make out, but eventually, I can sort through the rabble.

'...that old serpent, who is called the devil and Satan, who seduceth the whole world...'

That's me. As I lay on my back in the mossy earth, a peal of cackling laughter reverberates back from the endless expanse of trees, emanating from my mouth, and ringing back against my eardrums.

I am the Devil, I am Lucifer, I am Satan. This is my punishment, this is my never-ending remorse, this is my repentance, and Liache? Well, she was fated from the beginning. A consolation prize because once upon a time, I was God's favorite, and He still loves me.

Liache is my gift, she is my punishment. He wants me taken care of because He knows I can't take care of myself and wants me to feel every ounce of pain that this life will give me.

I lay on the moss and muse to myself about this, I drift into technicolor dreams of nonsense, white rabbits, giant dragons, morphing, colorful skies and angels and demons.

When I wake up in the morning, Liache is already awake and in the kitchen making the feast she always makes the morning we leave. Her and I normally have a better night than last night, but it's fine. I get dressed and kiss her cheek before I haul my bags outside.

For whatever variant reason, our first show of the tour will be no less than an eternity's drive away from where all of us live. Fucking assholes.

When we're all done eating breakfast, the kitchen looks like it has been ravaged by a full army of starving men. This is why they all love her so much, the fact that she takes care of all of us like it's her job, like she's, our mother. She has her own brand of insanity, her own problems, but she's always put this in front of everything else, she's always supported this dream for all of us.

Right now, Gabriel is yelling at me from the driver's seat of the bus that if we don't leave right now, we're not going to make it to the first damn show on time, and I couldn't really care any less. I kiss Liache gently, tell her to be safe, to be careful. She nods sweetly, and hugs tight. Too tight.

And that's it. That's the last time that I'm going to see her for the rest of the month. That's just the first leg. We'll be out for a month, back for a week, out for another three weeks, etc. That's just the way that this works. I'm glad that the tour will be punctuated, relieved by short visits home, but I'm frustrated that there's so much back-and-forth with this. Regardless, this is what we do, and it is incredible.

The people that we must deal with on the way to this are innumerable to me. It doesn't enter my little world because I can't take them, I can't snort them, and none of them provide me with drugs. Well, sometimes they do, but never consistently enough for me to give a flying fuck about them. There are bus drivers and managers and label executives and all the sponsors, oh the sponsors. This energy drink, that shoe company, this guitar company, that drum company, there are liquors and makeup companies abound, and all of them want to give us something. As long as I can buy drugs, I told the boys, I don't care what happens. I'll do what I have to do in order to continue my supply. On that day, not a single fuck was given.

This might feed into the idea that I'm an incredibly selfish person, that I don't care about anybody unless they fall into my little universe, and that is very, very true. I hate everybody, I hate everything, and I am actively working towards my own destruction because fuck you, nobody gets to tell me what to do but me, and I have chosen this specific set of criteria.

Out here, on the road, on the way to my first show, I am my own person. I am away from Liache, away from any petty bullshit, and surrounded by only petty bullshit, and I love it. I am hustling in the worst possible way, and I love everything about it.

We've been on the road for a few hours now and Marc, Luc, and I are already off our asses on whatever Luc decided to grace the bus with. The first show is in Nowhere, Arizona, or maybe it was Nevada. I don't care. I'm not the one who drives. Or any of the various people who do that.

Roadies and light and sound technicians and every conceivable various professional that we might need set to work as we struggle to pull ourselves together. Gabriel has never been a part of this, but Marc and Luc like to play a game they affectionately call 'get the singer as fucked up as we can and see how badly the first show goes'. I'm more than a little bit okay with this. In fact, I love the idea that just a few weeks ago, Marc was lecturing me on the number of drugs that I do, and here he is now, encouraging my consumption as rabidly as his little brother. It's an interesting phenomenon, what happens to us on the road.

The first show goes about as well as you can expect it to go before, I'm fully acclimated to operating on this level of fucked up consistently again.

I barely notice any of the opening acts that come before us at this small venue in the middle of nowhere, as far as I'm concerned. At some point during the show, I lose my balance at the edge of the stage. I've misjudged the distance between me and the rather porous crowd at the front of the stage, and, miraculously, the small group of people manages to catch me, and shove me back onto my feet on the stage.

"Fuck yeah!" I shout into the microphone, eliciting an uproarious cheer. "I don't know where the fuck we are, but you guys rock!" More shouts of agreement, a deafening cry of unity in an otherwise tumultuous time in history.

I launch back into the lyrics, finding my feet on this stage, and I might as well be back at the practice hall. I am blissfully ignorant of the thousands of eyes upon me at this instant, the people who have come from miles around just to see this show, just to see us, just to see me. This feeds so heavily into my narcissism, my ego, that I genuinely fear that I won't come back from this, but that happens every show. The chorus of shrieks melts into the music and lifts me higher, dragging me into insanity. Adrenaline pumps through my veins as I turn to look out over the sea of people. Huh, there's more now, the spaces between the people are smaller. Somewhere off to my left, there's some asshole with a camera, clearly filming the whole thing. I laugh between songs, flipping him off casually as the deep, amused chuckle rolls out over the crowd from the amplifiers.

I feel so much larger than life. This is the closest to Heaven that I'll ever be. It is more addictive than any substance I know, and I'm not letting it go, not ever.

The cheers invigorate me and send me spiraling down a path of addiction, of pain and suffering, and hard work and terrible, debilitating amounts of fun. I am surrounded by yes men, enablers, and suppliers, the kind of people who just want to have a good time while they're doing back-breaking labor and will do anything to achieve that. It is for this reason that within a week of being on the road, I'm nursing a severe addiction. Almost every night is a new show in a new place, punctuated by 20-hour stints of what should be sleeping or preparing but is usually just me getting incredibly high and occasionally hauling shit around with the roadies. In fact, at this point, I'm pretty sure I'm not actually allowed to do anything else. If I did, we'd probably end up in Malaysia or Middle Earth or some shit. All the eyes might be on me publicly, but if I were to say there was a 'leader' of our little band, it was Gabriel.

Gabriel was the first to take the lead on the drum company issue, and it just escalated from there. Soon enough he was having discussions with Marc and Luc about their respective preferences, and he took the head on that one, as well.

If Gabriel ever talked to me about sponsorships or record labels or contracts, I barely remembered any of it. Eventually, he learned to dumb it down for me. He would ask if I wanted more money for drugs, and if I answered yes (and I always answered yes), he would simply get me to sign whatever paperwork was necessary and then direct me to do the variant task associated with that paperwork, or if possible, he would just do it for me. Gabriel did all the actual heavy lifting while the rest of us were being useless. Gabriel made sure the dream happened while the rest of us were busy living it, he maintained it.

This is why it hurts me so much to think that he would be actively trying to get closer to Liache. This is why it feels so much like betrayal. Knowing that he's out here with me while she's back at home brings me an insane amount of comfort.

Luc and I are becoming closer as the tour progresses. We are doing a lot of drugs with any and all of the users from the other bands on the tour, the roadies, and a handful of awesome fans after each show. Life is amazing, it is a giant party and there's nothing to slow our momentum, nothing to slow our steady supply of drugs, of people to do them with, of time. There's nothing that's interrupting us as we slug through the day-to-day of being on tour. Go here, do this, go here, get that, we need gas, we need to set up, we need this or that or these, and it all sounds so boring, but when we're high? When we're high everything is a blast. Every day is a Saturday morning, and we have countless hours to get everything done and a bottomless amount of energy with which to do it.

It is brought to our attention at some point that in this town, Wherever, Colorado, they have this crazy cosmic bowling alley that this kid with us works at, in fact, he has the fucking keys to the place. It's about three o'clock in the morning, the place has been closed for hours, they don't really have a security team, and this kid, all he has to do is mention it and Luc and I are all about it. Suddenly, this is the entire purpose in life, this is the end-all and be-all of fun, this is the most important thing on our plates right at this moment. And we absolutely have to go, right now.

This little dude could not have been a day over 18, though his ID says that he's 27. There's no way that's true. He's too little and gangly. Still has growing to do. He brings us to his place of employment and turns on all the crazy black lights and me and Luc marvel at the intricate designs painted on the walls.

Planets, galaxies, entire universes unfold before us on the surfaces of this building. Some of these things, like the ones on the floor, well they're clearly tracked fluids, and that might be the grossest thing ever, but the intricacies on the walls, on the ceilings, which was the work of an artist. The pure insanity of this place seeps into my very pores as the giggles of the people we're with reverberating off the walls and simultaneously expand and limit the amount of space that we seem to occupy.

"*Le grand loup, nous devrions jouer*," I hear concrete evidence that Luc is more messed up than I thought when he slips completely into French. That's never happened before, not to this extent. He seems to catch himself, though, correcting so that I could understand. "Let's play, we should play."

Everything seems so incredibly hectic, but I oblige. There's nothing wrong with bowling a few rounds when you're in a place as awesome as this. The drugs work with the lighting to completely wreck my comprehension of the situation, the ball seems to float down on some fourth-dimensional pathway that I can't see before a full strike causes all the pins to fall in a thunderclap of epic proportions. Everything seems so much more visual right now like the sound is creating waves that I can see, but nobody else seems to be able to.

We are few, but still, the people we are with seem to be making an unprecedented amount of noise. This concerns me because this place is supposed to be closed, there's no room for error in a situation like this. More than half of us is carrying illegal drugs, and we still have a lot of fucking work to do.

Amazingly enough, I play against almost everybody that's here with us, and I win most of the games. It isn't until I begin throwing bowling balls through the air like a shot put that anything particularly alarming happens.

Flashlights are spotted through the tinted windows on the front doors of this place. Everybody immediately stops, it's silent for a moment until we hear the officer's radio, muffled through the closed doors. Every single one of us makes a break for the back door, leaving clear signs of our presence behind. While a thousand people will recount these a thousand different times with varying degrees of digression, not a single other person will actually believe them.

Over the next two weeks, I begin to hear more and more ridiculous rumors from the people attending my shows. George heard from his sister's husband that I replaced all the blood in my body with heroin so that I wouldn't go through withdrawals, Jason heard from some girl in his college class that I dyed my irises so that they would be this weird, frozen shade of blue. Never mind that I would be dead from an overdose if that were true, never mind that I would be blinded by my own stupidity. What really baffles me is that people believe this crazy shit. Someone told me that they heard I'd sold my soul to the Devil for the contract I'd gotten with the record label.

I laugh, heartily. Cackle, really. The laughter is forced out of my body in an almost violent outburst, and I look that kid square in the eyes, stop my laughter abruptly, and offer him a very twisted smile. I say, "I am the Devil," and I walk away without another word.

There is no doubt in my mind that he will never recover from that.

There's a week where we go home to prepare for the second leg of the tour, which means we've been gone for about a month. It confuses me, it doesn't feel at all like it's been that long, but the drugs we've been doing, the hallucinations I've been having have thrown off my perception of time. It's all just a haze of partying with opening acts and fans and being a fucking rock star, breaking into bowling alleys, and getting fucked up with the locals.

I barely comprehend that we are home. During the days, I try to recover from the night before, and during the evening, I'm trying desperately to get Liache to do my drugs with me. She obliges, but only sometimes. On the nights that she does, it is exquisite.

We are walking through the forest for what seems like the millionth time, hand in hand, happy. I am still jealous, and I am still suspicious of Gabriel, but to compensate, I stay by Liache's side like a lost puppy. There is a slight rain and due to the filter that the drugs have put over my eyes, I could swear that it's drizzling emeralds. The fairies are back and so are her illustrious wings. They are made of every color visible to the naked eye, and several that aren't. She is truly my angel, and I'm blessed to have warranted such a reward in this life. God knows I don't deserve it.

For a second, I think that we can have a normal life, that we can get married, have a family, and grow old together, and I realize that I've already convinced myself of it, I live and breathe the idea of it and it's what keeps me trying to stay alive. If I didn't have the belief, or at least the distant goal, I would probably go completely insane. I realize that I honestly believe that once I'm done this life, once I'm too old to do this every day, we'll be able to have a life.

I kiss her gently, breathing in everything that she is. All the light, the earthy, heavenly scent that surrounds her, the joy, the music, I can feel it inside of me, it's like the love of God, that ever-present and ever-evasive love of our parent that we strive for. I drag her by the hand back to the house, the entire time she's almost protesting, asking what we're doing. I don't answer, just keep walking.

I'm making an impulse decision.

I'm probably going to regret this later.

I throw her onto my bed, our bed. I pin her down and I kiss her again. My heart is racing, and so is hers, but for two totally different reasons. I revel in the fact that I can elicit this kind of feral response from her while I search my pocket for something I've been carrying since the day I met her. My right hand finds her left, and upon her finger, I slip a dainty silver ring. It is small and intricate, inlaid with amethyst. Her bright green eyes widen, her pupils dilate, and she gasps ever so quietly before I lean in to whisper in her ear.

"We're getting married when I get back." It is not a question, it is a statement, and it is very nearly a command.

Liache takes the lead from here, and we spend the night intoxicated, in the throes of passion.

I don't think anybody knows how long I've had that ring, or even that I had it at all, but I knew the moment that I met her, she was going to be the woman I spent the rest of my life with.

Unfortunately, we are leaving once again the next day, so I don't get to enjoy the beaming, constant excitement as she essentially completely plans our wedding. I know it will be beautiful, and perfect, because it's her. Maybe this is my path to redemption, maybe I can repent through accepting the gift that was given to me.

I haven't told anybody because it's none of their business anyway, but it doesn't stop Gabriel from noticing the ring on her finger. He notices things like that, it's strange to me because I'm not particularly perceptive. Well not most of the time.

Sometime later, after we've been on the road long enough for me and Marc and Luc to be high again, he asks me about it.

"Did you ask Liache to marry you?" he asks, his inflection is pure curiosity, he seems to just want to know what's going on in my life, but I know better.

Still, I'm not going to be an asshole about it. "I didn't ask. I informed."

He scoffs. "You really are a hopeless romantic," he laughs gently and stands up. "I'm happy for you, dude." He's over it now, he disappears elsewhere on the bus to read his stupid book or something equally intellectual. He's always been that way, introverted, control-freakish, nerdy. He still seems like that shy young man who is terrified of talking to girls, but he's comfortable with Liache. Maybe that's what sets me on edge?

Luc laughs quietly from the seat beside me. It's not so much a laugh as it is a single, broken up sigh. "Congratulations," he says at the end of his soft chuckle. Something about his demeanor says that he is feeling the same way about my marriage as he does about Marc having found Ann.

Marc, on the other hand, seems disinterested. Maybe it got him thinking about marriage, children, a personal future. He doesn't really seem like the type of person that would multitask this and having a personal life, a family, he seems like the kind of guy who would tell his grown children of the times he was on the road with their crazy Uncle Luc, his eyes glossing over with nostalgia as he wonders whether or not me or Gabriel ever settled down. But who am I to say? Maybe he went into panic mode, fearing commitment like any normal young adult male. Maybe I'm wrong about him, maybe we're in for some craziness when his inner rock star is released.

It is impossibly hot today. We're somewhere in Wisconsin, and me and Luc are floating down one of those lazy rivers in some water park, holding onto each other's inner-tubes, drinking from flasks we definitely smuggled in. Not that we needed it, we were already all kinds of fucked up.

"How do you know?" Luc asks, with no real sign one way or the other what on earth he was talking about, not to mention breaking a perfect silence in a crowded recreation area. "Like, is it some divine interference, some kind of sixth sense, some conscious decision? How do you know when you are ready to get married?"

A chuckle escapes me. What a terribly strange thing to ask. "I don't think it's a ready thing," I respond in an even and measured tone. Trying to organize my thoughts into actual speech at this level of intoxication, with a subject as intangible as this is proving difficult for me. "I think it's a gamble thing. I mean, I'm just not willing to face the idea of a life without Liache, so I'm doing what I feel like I need to do to keep her around." That made me sound terrible, let's try that again. "Or wait, no, I need her, and I need her to know that, so I'm vowing to spend the rest of my life with her?"

Luc bursts out into a fit of laughter, and I mean a fit, and I realize that I absolutely do not deserve her. I'll do better when I'm back at home, I'll do better when I have her to keep me sober.

"*Tabarnak*, you are the worst," Luc giggles to himself. "I am amazed she still wants anything to do with you."

"That's fair."

Luc groans loudly. "I'm bored, it's boring here, let's go do something." He gets off his inner-tube and wades to the side of the 'river', climbing out easily. I follow suit, and we're off to the place with the bar. There's one around here somewhere, we saw it already.

Once more, completely wasted, we are still miraculously being served. The few incredibly alcoholic, unbelievably fruity drinks I've had put me over the edge, everything in life seems like it's being filtered through several layers of gauze, and I can't figure out if it's me that's moving in slow motion, or everybody else. Or the air just got thicker? I really can't tell. Everything is like a dream. My movements are sluggish, my reactions are slow, the world looks to me like I'm wearing dirty glasses. I take my sunglasses off to clean them several times, and when nothing works, I give up and just leave them on my face. At the very least I know they're hiding how impaired I actually am.

It seems like within milliseconds, Luc had a drink spilled all over him, somebody was bleeding, my hand hurt, and we were being carted out of the water park by big, burly men. The pavement scrapes several layers of skin from my elbows and hands as I stop my face from hitting the ground. Luc was less successful, I can see when I turn my head to look at him that he has blood running from his nose down over his mouth and chin, but not much else.

I collapse on the ground in laughter. I can't stop. At least not willingly. As I'm pulling myself up off the ground, rising slowly to my feet and trying to stand, desperately trying to stand,

I hear Gabriel's voice.

"I gotta go, Liache, they just got back from the park."

Of course, his choice to not use the term 'kicked out' was mostly to shield Liache from the craziness that happens when we're on tour, but I'm pretty sure she knows at least that we're fucked up. It's fine, she knows us. At least neither of us got seriously injured.

Gabriel gives us that look, that dad look, that 'why am I still cleaning up after you' look and gets back onto the bus. We follow, and now we're back on the road.

For whatever reason, he always does put up with our shit. He puts up with Luc and his girls, and our drugs, and our drinking and hanging out with the fans. I wonder, while watching buildings get replaced by trees get replaced by open farmland in my window, whether this is sustainable. Logically, I know it isn't, but I want it to be, with all my heart I pray that this is sustainable. I love it.

I start to realize, as time passes on this eternity of a tour, that Gabriel is spending an awful lot of time on the phone with Liache. It seems like every time we come back from doing something, anything at all that's extraneous, he's on the phone with her. The first few times, I would look at my phone and see an absurd number of missed calls from her, but eventually she just stopped bothering. She would just phone him instead, because she knew I wouldn't answer my phone.

This is highly upsetting to me. The scenarios in my head go wild, and over time, I become frustrated, a bitter mess of anger and deceit. Time becomes a mess of drugs, and I don't even remember the next time we hit home to start the next leg of the tour.

It is counter-intuitive, but I spend every moment of every day with Luc in my self-loathing. We start to fuck with Gabriel, leaving small piles of drugs on his pillow, sometimes lumps of wet toilet paper.

At some point we cross the border into Canada, and a few days of constant driving and shows and blurred, distorted time later, Luc and Marc load up on food that nobody's going to eat simply because they can't find it at home. Shit that I can barely pronounce, cretons, tourtiere, oreilles de Crisse, some mess of cheese and gravy and french fries, poutine? We must be in Quebec somewhere.

The brothers are obviously happy to be home, but I'm quickly growing tired of having food shoved into my mouth. It is thick and greasy, and I can feel it clogging my pores, my arteries the second it enters my mouth. It's all carbs and varying degrees of animal fat slathered onto something reminiscent of sustenance.

The French have terribly fattening food.

What they didn't prepare me for, however, was how hard the people here like to party. While we're here, in what I'm now assuming is Quebec City, we play this shitty little bar venue. It's definitely smaller than the gigs we get back at home, but it's something, and it's good. The crowd here is particularly excitable, there are drugs everywhere, the people are snide and rude and screaming things in French while Marc and Luc obviously start to take offense.

It must be the regulars at the bar that don't know who we are, because several of the actual fans out in the crowd start throwing punches in the most brutal fucking mosh pit I've ever seen in my life.

Say what you will about the people here, the separatists, the ones who are rude to anglophones, who know English and refuse to speak it, the people in Quebec are passionate. Unapologetic and vulgar from what I've seen, yes, but they are full of piss and vinegar. In fact, the culture and attitude are so different here from the rest of North America, that I feel like I've completely left the continent.

I'm watching this throng of absolute chaos from the stage, reveling in it completely, loving and absorbing all the anger and confusion, and still managing to sing. I'm still managing to hold myself together above all the drugs and the noise and the increasing entropy before me.

Until someone throws something hard and glass.

Until somebody shatters a beer bottle across the stage.

Until that beer bottle strikes Luc in the fucking head.

In an instant, I'm down in the thriving concourse, throwing punches with the best of them.

This has very quickly degenerated into a riot. This has very quickly become a problem. I feel Gabriel's strong arms around my rib cage, pulling me away from the danger, from the impending assault charges, from the mass of people that the bouncers are struggling to control, and failing utterly. That's our cue to leave.

It may not have been legally advisable, it might not have been the best idea, but we manage to pack up and leave before the police are called. We're only three hours from the border, our next show is in Vermont.

"*Crisse d'osti*, the maple syrup 'ere is terrible," Marc's voice rings out at me from across the table at this little greasy spoon of a breakfast place. I'm amazed he's eating. "We were spoiled at 'ome, ah Luc?"

"*Oui*," Luc's response sounds more like a quack than my understanding of the French word for 'yes', but I pick it up regardless. He's too busy shoving food into his mouth to say anything further.

We're somewhere in Buttfuck, New Hampshire, and I am lazily pushing breakfast sausage around my plate instead of eating. Gabriel is pacing outside the large windows of this establishment while on the phone. The rest of everybody has found their way to other restaurants in the little plaza. Away from me.

I feel like that's fair at this point. I'm bitter and frustrated and irritable and my dislike of Gabriel is toiling away beneath the surface of my skin, damaging from the inside, threatening to dissolve it completely and leave me exposed. I know he is on the phone with Liache. It seems like he's been on the phone with her since we left, and that really burns my ass.

It seems like no matter how far we come, no matter how geographically far away we get from her, no matter how much I had healed from the last episode of toxic suspicions, he keeps getting on the phone with her and setting me off.

I haven't been easy to deal with. I know it, and Luc and Marc are too intoxicated to see it, because they haven't been my targets. The people I don't know, sometimes the fans, but largely Gabriel, have all been my targets. The roadies, the screaming, rabid concertgoers, the drummer in our own fucking band, they're all fair game.

I am sick of being crammed like sardines on this stupid fucking tour bus, I'm sick of being away from my fiancé, I'm sick of my alleged best friend being on the phone with her day and night. This stupid tiny fucking bunk under somebody else's stupid tiny fucking bunk is barely enough room to breathe, let alone to move around or try to actually sleep in. This constant, compounding misery is currently why I hate everyone and everything. I feel like a blocked pipe, my emotions acting as a constantly building fluid pressure, threatening to warp and bend the metal of my psyche until finally, it bursts. But I'm bursting slowly, in increments. A fan says or does something I don't like while we're partying after the show, I'm going to punch him in the face. Maybe it's just misplaced aggression, because the only person I want to punch in the face is outside pacing and on the phone with my future wife.

I stand up from the table, sending my plate clattering loudly to the floor as I do, and head directly to the door. I purposely knock into Gabriel with my shoulder as I walk past him and onto the bus. I'm done, and I'm ready to move on, which realistically means I'll be waiting on this bus, stewing in my own misery until everybody else is done doing what they need to do here. In the meantime, I'm going to be doing the drugs that I have, regardless of the rules we have set forth.

I just don't fucking care, I need to drown whatever the hell is going on in my head right now.

By the time we get moving to our next show, I'm so out of it that I can't feel my own face.

I've become so engrossed in my routine of; get fucked up, go here, move this, go there, lift that, take that apart, load it onto a vehicle, that I completely lose track of where we are in the country, or what day it is. Not that this is anything new.

Despite my drug intake, I've built some muscle lugging around the equipment with the roadies. It keeps me busy, keeps me from my impending violent outburst. The incredible explosion that's about to take place.

Tick.

Tick.

Tick.

I know we haven't gone far, it's cold here. I hate the fucking cold. And of course, the tour bus broke down in the middle of said cold area. I can't be sure where we are. I don't know much about the area or the time of year, but I know it's too early to be this cold. There's snow on the ground for Christ's sake. But we're coming up on the end of the tour, so we can't be far from home.

Luc and Marc are sitting with me, early in the day in some dive bar in the middle of nowhere, openly snorting drugs off the table. This is the point we've gotten to; this is the level to which we have sunk. Everybody but the three of us are all on their phones, trying to get a hold of somebody to fix the bus. It's harder than you'd think. Which is why we want nothing to do with it.

I prefer to let people buzz around me, letting me know when to be where and what to do. It's easier that way, there's less of a chance I'll screw things up. It's a lot easier for me to find drugs in a town than it is for me to find legitimate services.

I go outside for a smoke, the chatter of everyone just trying to find a competent mechanic drifts around my head, in one ear and out of the other, numbing my senses. The burning in my throat and lungs is a relief. It is immediate and glorious, and I wouldn't give it up for the world.

In amongst all the chatter, something sticks.

I hear the most beautiful name I've ever heard, but it's leaving the lips of my best friend.

Tick.

Tick.

I look over, and the blush on his cheeks from the cold, the frustration in his voice from the broken-down bus, the relief that seeps into his tones while he speaks with her, it's enough to drive me insane.

I know I'm terrible, and I know I should be better at answering my phone, but do they have to rub it in at every chance? I swear I can hear it in his voice, he loves her.

I can almost see the emotion dripping off his tongue while

he tells her to take care of herself, the pink aura that inevitably surrounds a man in love, the syrup oozing off his words as they float in the air, giant and perverse and inherently offensive to me. Only to me.

Tick.

"You too," he says into the receiver quietly as I take several measured steps toward him. I scratch my cheek nonchalantly, exaggerating all my movements and snickering quietly to myself, watching his face contort into mild confusion at my demeanor.

Without warning, I haul back and punch him as hard as I can.

Boom.

My world goes completely red, I have no control over myself, and no recollection of what is happening, even as it's happening.

The next thing I know, I've been sequestered onto the bus. I laugh. There is blood on my hands, my knuckles are busted open, and my hands are aching, bruised, and swollen.

This is perfect misery. I've hit the bottom, nowhere to go from here but up. My addiction, my paranoia, my self-loathing has gotten the better of me.

Gabriel walks onto the bus, his face is a busted mess compared to the chiseled, handsome, godlike countenance he normally sports, but he still manages to look better than me. He always does.

"What the hell is wrong with you?" his voice cracks over the silence between us like a whip. "Why the hell did you attack me like that?"

I scoff and shove past him, stepping down off the bus to go chain smoke until we must leave.

He knows what he's done.

"What the actual fuck, dude?" Gabriel calls from the door of the bus, a few seconds after I'd stepped off. Marc is dealing with the mechanic who finally showed up, but he sees the fury on Gabriel's face behind the growing bruise.

"Luc, get 'im the 'ell out of 'ere," Marc yells at his brother as he steps in front of an irate Gabriel.

Luc, without saying anything, keeps me walking. I put a cigarette in my mouth and reach for my lighter, only to find that Luc is already holding a flame to the end of it for me.

"Thanks," I mutter, quietly. There's no real tone to my voice, and certainly no hint of remorse. I hate everything this tour has become, I hate Gabriel, I hate myself, I hate how I feel like I've lost her. I'm still fuming.

I pull the toxic, thick smoke from my cigarette into my mouth, tasting every swirling flavor it has to offer my tastebuds before I breathe it down into my lungs, the burning sensation offering me only a modicum of relief. I suppose at the very least I'm starting to calm down.

Luc doesn't really seem to care why we fought, either that or he's figured it out on his own already. It's not like I've made any kind of secret to him just how paranoid I am about Gabriel and Liache. He might be the only one who knows, but I'm not sure.

Luc, however, knows exactly what to do. He's found me a shitty bar near the venue in which to continue drinking. He drags me into the restrooms there and lines up some of our drugs, then hands me a tenstrip of acid. He might be the best friend I've ever had. I pull as many tabs as I dare and drop them under my tongue. Counting has never really been my strong suit. I follow Luc's lead on snorting some of whateverthefuck-aine off the counters while the acid dissolves in my mouth, like the true drug connoisseur that I am.

Everything dissolves into my bloodstream, I can feel the different chemical compositions attacking my nervous system, altering my reality, my heart rate, my perception, all at the same time. The hallucinations, however, won't start for a little while longer. That works for me.

Luc and I head back to the bar and start doing shots. It's now probably late afternoon, because when we head back outside to smoke, we can see the lineup of people behind the venue we'll be playing at tonight hauling our shit into the building, setting up for a raunchy fucking night of awesomeness.

Suddenly, I'm stoked on life again.

This is going to be fucking awesome.

Somehow, Luc knows how to handle me. He knows I don't want to talk about it, I don't need to talk about it, I need to be distracted from it. I don't need to sit here and think about and process my issues with Gabriel and Liache because that will just lead to terrible decisions made later on in the night. It will just cause this caustic, nauseating, festering rot in my mind, a destructive fixation that isn't healthy for anybody, least of all me. That might not actually be true, it might be more dangerous to Gabriel's actual health, then again, he'll eventually hit me back.

There's another two hours before the show, if that. I'm not actually sure how much time has passed. Luc and I are just shooting the shit, talking about inconsequential crap, not realizing nor caring one way or the other that we should have been helping the roadies and everybody set everything up. At the very least, we should have been offering our patronage to the venue we would be playing that night, as opposed to the rival bar across the street.

Eventually, Luc leads me back across the street, still in an incredibly, impossibly, irrationally 'up' state. I'm still terribly angry, but I'm not thinking about it right now. And that's just the way it needs to be.

Now that everything is being set up, now that people have started to file into the building and drink, I decide I need to top up on my drug intake. I drag Luc back out to the bus, find my stash and we both imbibe, while I, of course, take another couple tabs of acid.

I hadn't actually realized how much my world had been swimming until now, when everything took an odd turn, the walls seemed to take on a more melted appearance as opposed to their previous beating, the sea of people seemed to be far more multi-colored than they had been before. Instead of the varying shades of tan, suddenly people are purple, pink, fluorescent yellow, and blue. And absolutely glowing.

I smile, feeling a little more than insane but completely comfortable. I'm content. I look like a maniac but I'm so at ease right now it's insane.

I guess it's time for us to take the stage. I wade through the throng of people between where I am at the bar and where I need to be at the stage, giving people high-fives, smiling like a maniac and pretending I know everybody.

We're mid-card on this tour. We fall somewhere in the middle of all the other bands, but I always feel like the headliner. Like I give a fuck about anybody that goes on stage after us. I mean, I'm cordial, and I usually hang around through their sets, but that's more or less fan service than it is anything else. I make other people feel important, and in turn, they buy my shit. And that then generates money for me to buy more drugs, and that's a cause I can get behind.

I finally get to where I need to be, and I know we're not quite up yet, so I disappear with the rest of my bandmates. Gabriel isn't saying anything to me. He doesn't usually before a show, so this doesn't strike me as terribly odd.

We finally break out onto the stage, and everything feels so incredibly theatrical to me. I waltz out, taking in every second of this wonderful gift, this perfect drug as it adds to the intoxication of the substances that I'm already on.

I fucking love this.

"How are all you fuckers doing tonight?" my voice rumbles low through the amps in a wave over the crowd. In response, I hear a resounding cheer from everybody in the building. "Well get ready to throw down because we are Babylon's Fall and we're here to fuck your shit up!"

More screams rise over the crowd, seeping into my psyche through what I'm sure are now perforated eardrums. I don't give a shit. We launch into the first song on the set, and I can't help but to notice that everybody here is singing my lyrics. The visuals on this, the drug induced synesthesia creates this beautiful image, makes their voices look like they're rising out of them like tissue paper flames on a children's puppet show.

Somewhere in this glowing mess, sometime in the middle of our set, I spot her in the crowd.

Liache must have made her way out here to see me.

Suddenly, that's all I can focus on. I lose the sight of her in the crowd, but this entire performance has become about her. She's the one bright spot in my life, the one person who can keep me going and fix the bullshit that I've been piling on myself since we started this fucking tour.

If she told me she didn't love Gabriel, if she told me that everything was all in my head, I'd believe her. I want her to tell me, I want to hear it, but I want to tell her, too.

After the show, Luc and I are doing more of our fan service, hanging out on a couch with a few fans, though as far as service goes, Luc is getting the most. He's been making out with this random girl for a while now, and as he stands up and follows her to a presumably more private location, he leaves a sparkling silver trail behind him in the air. He must be quite happy. He's the only one of us that seemed interested even for a second in entertaining one of our female fans.

I've been left to my own devices in this little booth near the back of the club. I've taken all the acid that I had and am now working on... I don't even know what this is. It doesn't matter. After a few more minutes, I get up and head outside for a cigarette, one I desperately need to drag my soul kicking and screaming back into my body. I can't really understand what's happening right now.

I feel both sluggish and light as air as I make my way through that back door to where the busses are parked, dragging hard on my cigarette as I struggle to light it.

A flame appears at the end, as if by magic, and I look up, following the arm that's attached to the fire until my eyes settle on her face.

The most beautiful face in the world.

"Hi," she says softly through parted lips the color of rose petals.

I take in the sight of her, swimming in my vision, a beautiful apparition of hope in my all too dark and festering reality right now. I don't even respond; I just kiss her and start pushing gently toward our tour bus. Everybody else is still in the club, selling merchandise, talking to fans, and in Luc's case, probably getting laid in a bathroom stall, so the bus is ours for now.

The loud, beating music of the band still playing in the club is floating around us, mimicking my heartbeat, muted slightly by the concrete of the building. It pounds against everything, and space seems infinite, truly infinite.

I toss my cigarette and get the door to the bus open, backing her up the stairs carefully and shoving her gently down the narrow corridor to the back of the bus, where the lone actual bed is, all the while allowing my hands to explore her body, stopping slightly at key points that elicit a reaction. The bed is wider than the bunks, and doesn't have anything on top of it, just lovely, patterned pillows and blankets that came with the bus when we got it.

I don't actually bother to undress, nor do I bother to undress her, I just watch hungrily, dropping my pants ever so slightly as she pulls her panties off from beneath her skirt, and then climb on top of her, finding my way into the sweet, warm nectar that is her.

I've missed her so much.

My darling Liache.

I spend my night with her in a hazy passion, surrounded by my hallucinations, my own illusions. The fairies float around us, mimicking us on any surface they can find, nestling in among the strands of her hair or laying out across the flat of her tummy, the small of her back.

Liache's darling voice desperately begs me for more as I watch the fairies flutter around her face, as I flip her over and see the tiny orgy taking place on her back, feeding into her desperate frenzy.

I scare them off as I let loose all the tension, all the anger and sexual frustration of the last however long, and they shake their tiny fists, cursing at me in a language I can't possibly hear let alone understand. Liache cries out her satisfaction as I reach my own climax and collapse beside her on the bed, kissing her face.

I've reached peak exhaustion; my eyes slam shut and stay that way for the rest of the night.

Everything is exquisite, it is perfect, and harmonious, and I sleep like a well-fed baby.

When my eyelids scrape open over my desert-like eyes, Liache isn't there and the bus is moving. Gabriel's seat beside the driver, pointedly ignoring me tells me that he's still not talking to me after I attacked him, and that's fine. I still feel like I won out.

I got to fuck my fiancé on the tour bus after our last show, and he didn't. I can see it burning a hole in his head, I can see the envy on his face.

Luc starts to tell me, excitedly, about the girl he ended up with the night before, how dirty and impossibly hot it was to hook up with a stranger because he was in a band.

That's why most men get into the industry.

For them, it's all about the women, the groupies, the crazy hot, sexually insane women who will literally throw their shirts at you while you're on stage. Panties too.

It's never been about that for me. Sure, the possibility is alluring, the idea that so many want me is intoxicating. What makes it better is that they can't have me.

I'm glad that Luc is happy, that he's excited about this. I'm glad that he's having fun. I'm a little more than disappointed with the way that everything has been going so far. I want my best friend back.

Gabriel keeps glancing over at me, still trying to pretend I'm not there, but clearly more than a little annoyed at my very existence.

We've been here before. I've absolutely done and said stupid shit and pissed him off before, but this seems way more extreme.

Something's wrong.

Like the men that we are, neither of us bring it up. The short drive passes without any form of communication. We make our way back home with silence toward one another. No more time off for lazing in water parks, but the constant, insane flow of drugs has been a godsend. Luc and I are more fucked than we've ever been.

There isn't a moment of sobriety for us, and when we finally get home, I can't even tell them what year it is. It doesn't matter to me anyway. I can't even see straight.

Luc and Marc head on their own way, each to their respective homes, but Gabriel follows me into my house after completely ignoring me for the rest of the ride.

The door slams shut behind me, rattling several of the

decorations hung on the walls. I turn around in shock and my eyes fall upon Gabriel, who is seething with anger. Liache's soft footsteps echo down the hallway as she strides towards us, more cautious now that she can sense the tension. Her curiosity seeps off her, easily picked up among the atmosphere of rage.

"Tell her what you did. Tell her what I saw you do."

I meet Gabriel's statement and infuriated gaze with a look of complete confusion. "What? About when I punched you?"

He scoffs and takes a breath, trying desperately to compose himself. "No, you fuck," his words cut through the silence like a red-hot knife through melting butter. "I will make you rue the day you were born if you don't tell her what happened right now."

Liache takes a tentative step forward, trying to get a better look at both of our faces. Her voice rings forth quietly, thick with confusion. "What is he talking about?"

"I don't know." My answer is truthful. I have no idea what he's talking about.

His fist whips forward, cracking me in the face so much harder than it ever has before. It sends me flying onto my own floor, in my own house.

"Her name is Laura," he shouts down at me, shaking with a blind fury I've never seen in him before. "All she wanted to do was see if she could bring her boss our contract so she could prove herself, and you fucked her. You brought her onto our bus, and you had sex with her." He sighs heavily, trying to compose himself, and failing. "I watched you push her onto that bus, I saw your hands all over her, and I could hear you. Everybody heard you."

I hear Liache's weight drop onto one of our couches as she sits, shocked, and everything starts to make sense, things start to fall into place in my head.

I look up at Gabriel, wide-eyed as the blood trickles down my face from a freshly broken nose. "I thought she was Liache," the words slip from my mouth without so much as an apology. I can't believe that actually happened, I can't believe that wasn't her. It was her, it had to be her. I search my memory for any traces of that reality, and I can't find one single thing to cling on to. Not one thing to justify what happened, or why.

Panic floods my entire body as I sit on the floor, in complete and utter shock. My heart threatens to bust out of my chest and tears well in my eyes as Liache just gets up and walks out of the door, into Gabriel's car.

"This is your rock bottom," he hisses at me, dragging me to my feet by the front of my blood-soaked shirt. "Get your shit together."

I should have known. The fairies never bother her, they'd never dare to touch her.

I couldn't see her wings.

What have I done?

3

I call Liache every day, and every day she ignores my calls. I send her messages, I stalk her social media, I reach out to her in every way I know how. I try to pick her up from her art classes, her writing workshops, I haven't touched anything of hers in the house since she left, and she hasn't been by to pick anything up. She's staying with Gabriel and that infuriates me to no end. My soul is on fire every second of every day and I can't douse it with anything, not the way I normally do.

Luc and I are still nursing incredible addictions. We've graduated from rookie rockstar drug users to full blown addicts. I can't function without them anymore. My daily cocktail of substances has grown to the point where I'll look down at what I've created and feel immortal. Like if I just do enough drugs consistently enough, nothing can kill me, because what I'm taking at any given moment should be able to drop an elephant.

But it doesn't drop me.

Eventually, I start to ease up on Liache, and spend more time with Luc. We still get together as a band, and I ignore Gabriel entirely. Marc has become our official go-between. He doesn't seem to mind, as long as work is still getting done and I keep his drug addled brother away from Ann. It works for me.

Everything in my life feels like it's being filtered through layers of cotton, everything is padded, foggy, soft. It feels a little bit like watching a movie, I'm watching these things happen, but I'm not really being affected by them. I'm helpless to stop the unfolding of these events, so why should I care one way or the other what's going on in anybody else's life.

I don't think I've been alone since she walked out that door. Now, every time I call and she doesn't answer, I head at once for Luc, wherever he is.

It's just such a night, the phone is assaulting my ear with that God forsaken, high pitched trill when Liache picks up the phone.

"Stop calling me."

My phone makes a series of descending tones to tell me she's hung up the phone. I miss the old click of phone receivers, there was something therapeutic about slamming down the phone after a particularly shitty conversation or throwing a flip phone at the wall just to watch it shatter apart, knowing that you could reassemble it and it would be just fine.

At least some progress is being made. She answered the phone this time. Eventually she'll let me speak, right? We've been through so much, eventually she has to let me speak to her.

I go to Luc's and he's ready for me, like he always is. A giant smile on his face, ready to welcome me into his home because I can't handle being alone at mine. I hate the emptiness of my bed; I hate the echoes of my house. It's not the place that makes it a home, not the decorations, the furniture or appliances, it's her.

It's not home when she's not there, and she's never there anymore.

I only go home from Luc's to change clothes and call her.

I need to fix this, but I don't know how. I'm not strong enough on my own.

To be fair, this angst and turmoil has been great for my productivity. I'm writing a lot of music, and our times together as a band are almost normal. For me, anyway.

Luc looks at me, his face is almost sad, but he's too high for that. His eyes are glassy, his lips are pulled into a nearly permanent, foreboding grin.

"*Nous avons...*" Luc starts speaking in French and corrects himself at once. Something that's been happening more and more often the more drugs we take. "We 'ave this thing today. We gotta go meet the guys somewhere to sign some stuff." His tone is distant, distracted.

"Alright," I meet his tone with my own, disconnected sounding voice. Whatever it is that we must do, I know neither of us are really interested, but it needs to be done.

Being the more sober of the two of us, I drive to our practice hall, where Gabriel has decided we need to conduct our business. I'm assuming because he can't trust me and Luc to find a new address and doesn't want us at his home, where Liache is. I can't slight him for it, I can't slight him for any of it.

I'm angry at him, no doubt. I'm furious, but I know that

he's just doing what he thinks he needs to do to keep her happy, and I can respect that. The only reason I'm as angry as I am is because I'm positive that he's using this as an opportunity. She's upset, she's away from me, and she's staying at his home. I have no doubt that she's been spending her nights in his bed, I can envision it so vividly that I might as well have actual footage of her on top of him.

We walk in, greeted by Gabriel, Marc, and two strangers. One of them, the woman, looks terribly familiar. Short, dark hair, a little meek looking. The other is a tall, blond man in a suit, holding a briefcase and looking awfully official.

Gabriel looks at the two of us, not in the slightest surprised by our appearances. "This is Scott, he is our lawyer," he says, speaking slowly so that we understand. He's being a dick, but I don't care. At least he's still taking care of us. "This lady is Laura, she wanted us to sign a record deal. It is good, you're signing it."

I give the two new people a sideways look before meeting Gabriel's scrutinizing glare. He makes me feel like a toddler being scolded, without any actual scolding happening. I know what I did, and the evidence is right there in the room with us. I can't believe we're signing this deal, with her.

"She didn't do anything wrong, asshole." Gabriel barks at me, seeing my hesitation and understanding why. "Sign the fucking paper."

I do as I'm told, and so does Luc. I'm sure that eventually there will be a rundown on what is expected of us, a schedule given, shit to film, photos to shoot, whatever.

Laura sheepishly scoots out of the hall as Scott thanks us and leaves himself. I'm a little confused, but I don't care enough to ask any questions. Somebody will tell me what to do and when to do it, and it will all be fine.

Around Gabriel, I haven't been acting as angry as I feel, but more like a guilty child. I might be suspicious and furious, but I know I did something horrible.

I'm every bit the monster I feared I was.

"We have a few local shows coming up in the next couple weeks," Gabriel announces, more to me and Luc than Marc. "We want to keep the momentum from the tour, so we're going to start preparing for another tour probably within the next six months. We are going to work with Laura and her record label to get our name out there and trending upwards. We're going to do this and you two are going to do as I say.

"We will be here, in this practice hall, once a week. At this time, on this day, and there will be no exceptions. If you fuck around, if you aren't here consistently, if you, for whatever variant reason, don't want to do the tour, you will be replaced at once, and that's not coming from me. That's coming from the label."

Both of us nod and take our places, prepared to go through the motions.

I must admit, it feels amazing to perform the new music I've been writing, and we're well over halfway through the track list for our next album. We've never worked this quickly before, never worked quite this well creatively. It's been an amazing outlet.

But it's not enough. Nothing is ever enough for me.

The practice breezes by in a haze of loud noises and bright, burning lights, and we're back at Luc's house. It's just the two of us and neither of us are going to drive anywhere again for at least the rest of the week. There's no way we're going to sober up enough.

We have our stipulations from Gabriel, and we intend to follow them, but that doesn't mean we're going to be responsible in the interim.

"*Loup*," Luc utters my nickname quietly from his upside-down spot on his couch, looking directly across to where I'm sitting. "Do you ever wonder if this is where we're supposed to be?"

"What do you mean?"

"I just feel like guys like us," he pauses thoughtfully for a moment, assessing the correct choice of words. "Good t'ings aren't supposed to 'appen to us." He sighs heavily. "We're not good people."

I scoff. "Nothing about this is good, Luc."

"*Quoi?*"

"Yeah, we have a record deal, and yeah, we're making a lot of money, but dude," I take a deep breath and hold it for a second as I watch him finally try to sit upright. "This situation is fucking garbage."

There's a moment of silence between us. Complete silence. There's no noise from outside the house, no music is playing, no television making the static ringing sound I know is actually a pretty severe case of tinnitus. In this moment of silence, I have a second of clarity, of lucidity.

Liache isn't a consolation prize from God for damning me in the first place, for casting me out, she's a punishment. That night with Laura, that wasn't an accident; it was fate. He meant for it to happen, He meant to hurt me like this.

We sit in silence for a long time as I reflect on the situation at hand, as I sit here and curse God for all that he's put me through. But with this destruction, this pain and torture, comes a new resolve.

Like a frustrated, rebellious teenager, I decide that I can change what God wants for me. I can show Him that I'm not what He thinks I am, I don't deserve what He thinks I deserve.

"Luc," I whisper into the silence, as if I'm afraid to speak too loudly for fear of being overheard. By whom, I'm not sure. "Do you believe in Hell?"

"I don't know what I believe in," his honesty is astounding, and clear. Painfully clear.

That's the sad thing about humanity. It makes us question whether we believe. I think we're born knowing what to believe, remembering that there's something greater than this life, but the years of programming erase it from our memories. I think that the reason that all the major faiths have similar stories is because something happened thousands of years ago, and the stories were told and retold so many times that some things were lost in translation.

I know that God is real, I know that there's some truth to the stories, but even I, in this existence, have forgotten.

"I think that's where we are."

Luc sighs at me, obviously over the heavy topic of conversation. "You're probably right."

I know what I must do to prove Him wrong, to take back what's mine, but tonight is not that night. I don't have the resolve, not yet. I haven't spent enough time wallowing in self-pity. I haven't spent enough time destroying myself.

I think my problem is that, when I started doing drugs, I was still at that age where your ability to process consequences isn't yet developed. That tender, formative age between childhood and adulthood, where most people make the most mistakes in their lives. I have this theory that the reason I can't stop, I can't just be a normal person and stop doing these drugs and hurting people is because I've already burned out that part of my brain with a special blend of cocaine and whatever else I could get my hands on.

I consider myself lucky that I have a friend like Luc. He's always been there for me in a way that most drug addicts aren't. I know that when shit hits the fan, he won't run away. I know that if I needed any real help from him, he would be there for me.

Luc is a good man with a terrible influence on his life. Luc is a good man with a terrible best friend. Luc is a good man who is close with the Devil.

At some point, I head back to my house to make my phone call to Liache and change my clothes. The distance between our homes is incredibly convenient, and I'm glad that it's Luc I've been bonding with over the past however long.

I'm so involved in my routine that I don't notice the woman sitting on my front steps until I've already tripped over her and ended up on the ground in front of her.

"Sorry," she says, quietly, as though it's something she utters often enough to be a reflex. "I need to talk to you about some things." Her voice is thick with a vocal fry that grates on my nerves more than anything I've ever experienced. It's that Laura girl.

I ignore her, but walk into my home, leaving the door open behind me. She follows, closing the door and clearing her throat before following me through the rest of my house up to my room, where I start to get undressed. I want a shower.

"I'm supposed to assess whether your drug use is going to be a problem at all, in light of the night we met…"

I finally set my eyes upon her, unimpressed and clearly annoyed. "What about it?"

She gapes at me for a second, trying to find words, or gather coherent thoughts before she finally figures it out. "I, um, I think, I mean, I know that you thought I was somebody else," she stumbles over her speech nervously before she manages to compose herself. "And I know that it was because of the drugs, I just need to know that they're not going to be a problem."

I laugh. It's deep and somewhat menacing, rolling out and gently caressing the space in between us.

"Laura," I say her name quietly, spitefully. "What are you really doing here?"

Her face flushes with a deep red blush, and it's terribly satisfying to me that I have this power over her.

"I'm just doing my job," she says, her confidence wavering as I move closer, backing her up against a wall.

What am I doing?

"Laura," I growl her name, low and quiet in her ear as her back thuds against the wall behind her. "What are you really doing here?"

Her pupils dilate, her face manages to find a deeper shade of red, and she's clearly bothered. It's exquisite. I can smell the conflicting emotions rolling off her in waves, mingled with the scents of her sickly-sweet perfume and her sweat. I watch as the intricate colors and shapes in her eyes change, pulling the edges of her pupils ever wider, her amber eyes flicking between my topless body and my icy gaze.

What am I doing?

Because of the drugs, I can see every change in her body in some role. The shy flush in her face as her confusion sets in, the dewy sweat rising on the surface of her skin, her blown pupils searching for something she can't name, the shallowness of her breath as she realizes that I'm right.

There's another reason that she came here today.

I can see her bosom shaking as her heart pounds beneath. She doesn't say anything, just searches my eyes for meaning. I am the stimulus, and I can see the chemical chain reaction I've set off in her body, how each one thing leads to the next and eventually ends in her shivering body and quick, shallow breathing.

What am I doing?

The corner of my mouth rises in an egotistical smirk before I lean forward, just enough to whisper in a low, rumbling baritone into her ear. My body is close enough to hers to feel her trembling heat, but not to touch it, my arm pressed intimidatingly against the wall above her head, where she has stiffly plastered herself, paralyzed by one emotion or another.

What am I doing?

"I think you came here today to prove to yourself that the night we met had nothing to do with you."

"What do you mean?" she asks, her voice quiet, uneven and shaky, her signature vocal fry replaced by an insecure, desperate tone.

She's so controlled by her emotions, by the feral nature that humans normally work so hard to deny. She's so imperfect, so superbly human, so unlike Liache.

I move slowly so that my lips are just in front of hers, about to gently brush the surface, and utter, cruelly, "You want me."

She gasps as our bodies finally make contact, while I still hold back the kiss that she so desperately longs for. "No, I don't."

I chuckle at her lie. "Then walk away."

As I move to take a step back and allow her to leave, she wraps her arms around my neck and pulls me back to her, kissing me with an urgency I've never felt from anybody.

Her dam had finally broken.

She pushes me back until we both tumble on my bed, her hands working deftly to remove any clothing that might be in her way.

I'd be lying if I said I wasn't enjoying this.

Nothing intrigues me more than the unpredictability of human nature. Nothing is more interesting to me than the idea that people can just completely lose control. And she had lost control.

Laura and I fight each other for dominance in my bed, in my room, in our "working relationship". Both of us are struggling for superiority, both of us trying to top in the best possible way. In the end, we are both naked and clawing for control. This isn't sex the way I'm used to experiencing it, it's something entirely new and it is borderline violent.

I bite her shoulder, earning an enraptured shout from her as I roll on top and pin her hands down. She can't get out of this anymore. I've won.

"You disgust me," I groan in her ear, expecting her to fight against me to leave--and I would let her.

But she doesn't. She seems to revel in it. Laura must really hate herself. She becomes clearly more heated, more desperate, and she starts fighting against me harder but only to regain the control she'd lost.

It doesn't work.

By the end of our night, we're both exhausted, bruised and probably bleeding. I'm more satisfied than ever. So much so that right now, I don't have any conflicted feelings on it. She disgusts me, she repulses me to the point that I'm fucking drawn to her. Or maybe it's because I'm drawn to her that I hate her so much.

"I'll be keeping an eye on your drug intake," she threatens.

"Get out."

She gets up and leaves, but I know that she just strutted out of here with all the power she could have in this situation. She got what she wanted, and she also got the answer to my drug intake.

I think she knows that I wouldn't be fucking her if I wasn't being self-destructive, if I didn't hate myself for the first time that it happened, if I didn't want to die because I was enduring a special kind of hell, a purgatory made just for me; a life without Liache.

I'm a fucking moron.

I have the shower that I meant to have several hours ago, get dressed and head back to Luc's.

I don't bother to phone Liache tonight.

I walk confidently into Luc's house, clearly in a state of unease. What I've done is so plainly all over me, she may as well have dropped me in blue dye and written it on my forehead in glow in the dark ink. It weighs so heavily on my conscience that I barely notice Luc sitting in his chair, offering me more drugs.

"Are you alright?" he asks, concern is vivid in his voice. "You were gone for a while."

"Laura was at my house."

"Oh?"

I stay silent, and I know he can gather what happened from that alone. I don't want to talk about it. I just want to start working to get back where I was before this fucking nightmare of a tour. But I'm still not strong enough.

"*Merde.*"

Yeah, he got it.

He stands up from his awkward position and walks towards me, handing me yet another indiscriminate amount of acid. "This is probably a terrible idea."

I smile widely up at him and tear off a chunk of the paper, shoving it into my mouth. I must look like a maniac. I wonder idly why it is that this drug brings me so much solace, why I always find so much comfort in something that is equal parts beautiful and terrifying. I love it, I love looking at the most inwardly dark places of myself, assessing all my hallucinations, knowing that they will wash over me until they slowly ebb away from me. It brings color and light and beauty into the hellish landscape of my life.

I've been put here for a reason, and I'm going to figure it out and make it my own.

One day, I'm going to rule the world.

Eventually, my reality peels away from me, leaving me in the dust, and I'm not sure if I'm awake or not anymore. There's a hazy, dreamlike quality to everything around me, and I'm standing beside Liache in her true form, between her and Laura in hers.

To my right, Liache is beautiful and ethereal, and her wings are on full display. Is that a halo I see?

To my left, Laura, in her sultry temptation, red light highlighting her every intoxicating curve.

"Why did you do it?" they ask, both in unison, Liache in

her beautiful, sing-song voice, and Laura in her disgusting, croaky drawl.

I can't answer. There's no voice for me to respond with, I'm frozen in a place that doesn't seem to exist. My heart begins to race, my thoughts wandering in various, horrifying directions that I just can't control in the least.

"Why did you do it?"

Luc's voice breaks through my dreamlike hallucinations and brings me crashing back down to Earth.

I gasp, trying to catch my breath and regain my bearings. I've completely forgotten where I even was, the shock of everything shot adrenaline through my system so quickly that I'm not hallucinating anymore. Well, maybe just a little bit.

"What do you mean?" I ask, all my words blending into one long one. I'm surprised he can even decipher my sluggish question.

"You said she was at your house," he explains, slowly. "But why did you do it?"

"I don't know man." I ponder on that for a few moments, still trying to recover from whatever the hell just happened to me. I sigh heavily. "I fucking hate her."

Luc laughs. He's clearly amused. "I get that."

I cast him a sideways glance. That's the strangest thing I've heard in a long time. Maybe that's just me, though. I've been with Liache, this perfect, wonderful, gorgeous woman for so long, and I've only ever had eyes for her.

I reposition myself in my seat and let my head roll back onto the cushion. I hate this. I hate her, I hate me, I hate being without Liache, I hate everything.

"She left her mark, ah?" Luc points directly at my neck and chuckles.

"Of course, she fucking did." I get up to go examine myself in the mirror and my shirt is sticking to my back as though it's wet. Shit, I'm bleeding.

"*Tabarnak,* she did a number on you," Luc says, now following me and tugging up the back of my shirt to assess the damage. "Worth it?"

"Worth it."

"*Crisse d'osti*, must have been something."

Luc dabs at the scratches on my back with rubbing alcohol while I assess the more visible damage. What a little bitch. Then again, I can't really say that I didn't leave her with similar evidence. We tore into each other.

Over the next few weeks, I return to my routine of getting wrecked at Luc's, heading home to shower, change, and call Liache once a day.

And every so often, Laura is waiting at my front door for me when I come back to do this routine.

Those are the days I don't call Liache.

Those are the days that I need to pretend that what I'm doing isn't despicable, that I'm not a monster. I am, though. I'm the ultimate monster.

I can justify the first time with Laura, at least in my head. I thought that she was Liache, and I know I'll never be able to convince anybody else of that, but I know it. Since then, though? I've continued to do this while working, albeit not very hard, to get back in contact with Liache, trying to tell her how much I miss her, how much I need her.

How can that be true when I'm actively spending this time, having this amazing sex with another woman?

"Laura," I mutter, half-asleep after one of our infamously violent sessions. "Why the fuck do you keep coming here?"

"Because I hate myself almost as much as you do," she responds, coherent and without a second's consideration.

"At least you're honest, I guess." I take a long drag off the cigarette I'm smoking, the immediate damage it does to my lungs giving me a glorious sense of relief.

"Spending time with you is what I do instead of destroying my body with drugs," she says, spitting the words like an accusation in my face before she begins dressing. She turns to me, a serious expression on her face. "Just let me know when you want to stop, I might be able to help you with your little addiction problem."

I scoff. "I'd sooner die."

Laura sighs, heavily, as though there's real emotion behind it. "You probably will."

I don't have a comeback for that, and she leaves without another word. I'm alone with that reality, that realization. I know that the road back to my Liache is paved by my recovery, but I'm not ready to do it.

I've lived with this crutch for so long, how am I supposed to go on without it?

I head immediately back to Luc's, a fire in my chest that can only be quenched by drugs. Lots and lots of drugs. I can't handle the anxiety I'm feeling, and I know exactly how to make it go away.

I stop calling Liache, I stop going back to my house. Luc and I seem to live together in increasing squalor, the only thing that matters to us is staying high and making all the little appointments Gabriel has for us. The practice hall, recording time, and before I know it, the album is done and he's talking to us about the next round of shows, starting to set up the next tour to promote it. Things are happening way too fast for me.

I'm beginning to realize, after all this has started to catch up with me, that time is actually passing, and I need to do something about my ridiculous life, my broken fucking relationships.

I need to be able to take the stage when I finally take over, and I'm not going to be able to do that if I keep this up. I'll be dead.

The next time I head home, it's Gabriel, and not Laura, sitting on my front steps waiting for me. This is becoming a theme.

"I've been trying to get a hold of you," he says. "We need to talk."

I nod and walk past him, opening my door and allowing him to walk in ahead of me. He takes a seat on the couch and looks at me, waiting for me to take a seat somewhere, too.

"Listen, I know you well enough to know when you're in trouble," he explains, his tough face breaking into an expression of deep concern. "And you're in trouble, so why don't you talk to me about it?"

"I have nothing to say to you."

He laughs. "I think you do."

"What, you want me to talk about how I was so fucked up on drugs that I thought some other woman was Liache?" My voice is rising as I get through my rant. A dam of my own has broken, now. "Or about how you decided that she was the woman we'd get to draw up the fucking record contract? My fiancé is living at your house, you fucking prick. Why don't you tell me more about how I'm doing?"

Despite myself, despite my rage, my pure, seething anger, there are tears escaping my eyes, rolling silently down my face and leaving cold, wet trails in their wake.

"Are you ready?" Gabriel asks simply, as if that's all it would take.

I've fixed my gaze upon the floor in front of me, and I nod. He doesn't respond in the least, and when I'm met with nothing but silence, I look up. He's gone, and there's no evidence to support the fact that he was ever here in the first place.

Fuck.

I take my shower, I change into some clean clothes, and I hop back in my car, regardless of everything. I need to reconvene.

I can't decide whether or not I'm insane. I can't decide whether or not everything in my life is terrible because I made it so or because that's what was willed for me. If my punishment is self-inflicted or if it's divine intervention.

I'm not sure how I got here, I don't remember the turns I made or even parking my car, but I find myself standing face to altar, on my knees in a church.

I'm looking up at Jesus in his eternal place on that cross and I can't help to think about how lucky these people are. That God sent his only begotten son to die for their sins, so they might be accepted into the kingdom of heaven, but I am doomed to this purgatory. These people, they have a get out of jail free card, all they must do is repent and they get to go home but they also don't realize it when Angels are in their midst, they don't realize it when the Devil is staring them in the face with literal temptation. They don't remember the glory of that kingdom, the pure and perfect love of the Father.

I've even remembered to genuflect and cross myself before sliding into the pew. I need help, I need guidance, and I'm not afraid to ask the very one who cast me out, even if my memory has been hampered by this very existence.

"Our father, who art in heaven," my voice is quiet and uneven, shaky and scared. "Hallowed be thy name," The Lord's prayer has a very different meaning coming from those who knew Him. "Thy Kingdom come, thy will be done on Earth as it is in Heaven," This is a prayer leaving the lips of a broken man, a prayer of remorse, of desperation. This is a true prayer of contrition. "Give us this day our daily bread and forgive us our trespasses, as we forgive those who trespass against us, and lead us not into temptation, but deliver us from evil…" My voice floats up and disappears into the frankincense infused darkness, seeming to just be absorbed into the night. "…for thine is the kingdom, the power, and the glory for ever and ever."

I sit in silence for a while, drinking in the serenity of this place. Any house of worship is a place truly touched by God, a place where people can go to get a little taste of home.

For me, this is torture. It reminds me of the vast, gaping chasm left in the absence of His love. It reminds me of how fucked up I truly am.

I kneel in this church, in this hallowed building where I clearly don't belong, and I pray to God who cast me out for strength. I pray to Him for courage, I pray to Him for guidance. As something completely out of character for me, I've come here seeking forgiveness. Nobody would have guessed it, but I am a penitent man. Instead of bashing my head against the invisible wall I've created for myself, I have opened myself up to the possibilities, the idea that I could live a sober and happy life. That if I could just get through this mess, if I could just stop acting like the spoiled brat that got kicked out of his home, then I could spare Liache the misery she doesn't deserve.

My phone starts to vibrate in my pocket, and I step outside. This place deserves at least that much respect. As I answer the call and raise the phone to my ear, Liache's annoyed voice lashes out at my eardrum.

"Now I can get you to answer the phone," she chides, bitterly. I don't respond. I understand what I've put her through, I know she has every right to be bitter and angry with me and she deserves every second of petty outburst. "You stopped calling."

"You told me to."

"Since when have you ever listened to me?"

I sigh and roll my head back, still holding the phone to my head as I reach with my free hand into my pocket for my cigarettes. "Why did you call me?"

"We need to talk."

"Is it weird that I've been dying to hear those words?"

"Just shut up and come see me," she says before she hangs up the phone. I can hear the smile in her voice, she missed my stupid hassling.

It takes me a second to absorb what she's said, but once it processes, I'm in my car and on my way to Gabriel's house. I can't believe that she actually called me back. After all the times I'd called her since she left and finally, now that I'd stopped calling her, she wants to talk.

I'd like to think that I was purposely giving her space, but I know damn well that I was distracted by Laura. I know that I was being a terrible person doing depraved things to another broken human being. Either way, I'm glad she called.

I pull up to Gabriel's house just as he's leaving. He casts me an angry glare and knocks his shoulder into mine before getting into his own car. My eyebrows knit in confusion over my reflective sunglasses before I walk through the door, greeted at once by a large sweatshirt clad, puffy-faced Liache. She cracks a weak smile and turns, leading me down a hallway to the bedroom she's been staying in.

She drops her weight heavily onto the bed, one leg curled beneath her as I sit in a computer chair across from her. I don't want to assume too much right now. This is an incredibly delicate situation, she's fragile right now.

"Don't say anything. Just, actually listen to me for once." She sighs, looking past the end of her knee and at the floor instead of at me. "I hate what happened. I hate that there's another woman and I hate that it hurt me so much. But what I hate the most is that I know it wasn't like you to do something so stupid. I know you better than to think that you would hurt me like that."

89

"Liache, I wou--"

"Shut up." She closes her eyes, a small tear escaping as she struggles to hold herself together. I listen, paying closer attention to how she is now. Her hands are shaking, her voice is uneven, and she's clearly struggling to sort out her thoughts. "You have to get clean. Do you hear me? I need you to do that for me because I can't do this anymore. I can't keep waiting for you to sort your shit out while you get fucked up and almost die or too fucked up to tell if that's me or somebody else…" A sob escapes her here and she buries her face in her hands for a second. She takes a deep breath and drops her hands in her lap, looking up at the ceiling in an attempt to keep the tears from falling. "The messed-up thing is that I still love you. I don't care what's happened between then and now, I don't give a shit. I can't imagine my life without you, but I can't take any more of your shit."

I slide across the gap between us, sitting beside her on the bed and I wipe the tears from her cheeks. She laughs, weakly.

"I will check into rehab tomorrow if that's what you want from me."

Liache nods and wraps her arms around my neck. "I missed you so much."

"I missed you too, sweetheart."

As we embrace, I begin to kiss her neck gently. I'm not sure what I'm doing, if it's just familiar, if I'm on autopilot, or if this is what's meant to be. I kiss up the side of her neck, across her cheek and toward her beautiful lips.

The next few minutes are a wild confusion of senses. The smell of her skin, the heat of her breath, the taste of her lips against mine. It's been so long since we were together, since we were amicably in the same room, that neither of us can control ourselves, and before I know it, we're caught in the throes of passion.

I don't enter into this lightly. I know that every touch and every kiss is a promise. This is a promise to get clean, to treat her the way she deserves, to take care of myself.

This is so different than anything I've experienced before, even with her. This is passionate, deep, and emotionally loaded.

It's as if I've always taken her for granted, that my knowledge of who and what she is, that she was made for me has sullied any earlier experience. This is raw emotion; this is something that only her and I could know. This is love.

I'm not sure how we got from her tears to post-coital bliss, but I'm not complaining, either.

Liache doesn't want to have any major conversations until after I'm out of the program, and I feel like that's fair. I've been fucking around for so long that I feel like I owe her this one.

I take my leave and as I step out into the bright sunlight, the weight of the world drops uncomfortably onto my shoulders. I start to realize the importance of the promises I've just made, and I start to panic a little bit.

I look at the clock on my dash and see that it's noon. I realize why this day seems like it's taking so long; I haven't slept. Last night, in the wee hours of the morning, I went to a church, and I prayed for what was hours, and then Liache phoned me this morning. Time feels unimportant, like it's just there as a minor inconvenience, and I realize now that when I said I'd check into rehab tomorrow, it meant tomorrow. I have a day to prepare myself for that reality, and that's overwhelming.

I'm back at my house, trying to pack, I guess. Take some clothes and put them in a bag to take with me to the nearest facility. Where that is and how much that'll cost, I'll figure it out later.

I figure I should get rid of my stash, and I'm having a hard time concentrating. It feels like there's wax paper between me and reality, something just fundamentally in my way. I can't quite lay my hands on anything at all. What better way to reinforce my concentration than to 'get rid' of all these drugs?

There's not actually a lot left. Just enough for right now. So, I do it all. It works out to a couple lines of coke and two tabs of acid, and I'm glad that I have this specific combination of drugs. I go back to sorting through my things and end up somehow in Liache's art room. Her in-home studio.

I walk around the walls and look at all the sketches she has pinned to the cork that she's covered almost all the surfaces in. Self-portrait sketches, preliminary sketches for surrealist, impressionist, renaissance style paintings. Stupid little doodles, outline illustrations for children's books. She's so talented.

I'm hung up on the sketch I could swear was Gabriel when Luc walks in.

"Does this look like Gabriel to you?" I ask him, without looking away.

He walks up slowly and ponders for a second, taking in the whole room before looking at the same sketch as me. "Yeah, little bit."

I wander back into my living room and sit on the couch, Luc following close behind. He plops down in the chair next to the couch and we both stare off into space for a little while.

The world starts to lose its consistency, some objects seem to melt away from their places on the walls, on the shelves.

"You ever think about the future?" he asks me, simply. "Like, where we will be in five, ten years?"

"Not until recently." We both continue to stare out in the same direction.

"What is it that you want from life?"

I close my eyes and ponder on his question. It seems so oddly pointed, so direct. Visions of Liache start to dance in the intricate show of phosphenes behind my eyelids. There she is, in all her glory. Every strand of her chestnut hair seems to bend to her very will, her perfect form beguiles me, charms me into this security, blankets me in this wonderful sense of… me. I can see our home, our wedding, our life and love play out like a movie projected into my mind, secret wants and needs that I alone can see.

"I want Liache."

"Then chase 'er, *Grand Loup*."

When I open my eyes, I am alone. Once more, I'm left with no evidence as to whether or not anybody else was ever here. How long have I been sitting here, hallucinating and fantasizing about my future, my life with Liache?

My phone rings, vibrating its way loudly across the table. I answer it, but before I can say anything, I hear Marc screaming on the other end.

"*Où es-tu, connard? Luc est mort, et toi, aussi!*"

"I can't--"

"*Crisse de calice d'osti de sacrement,* Luc is dead, *enfant de chienne*! You left 'im alone wit' a pile of fucking drugs, you fucking addict."

I have no voice with which to respond, and Marc grows tired of my silence.

"*Osti d'épais de marde, bâtard. Ne joue pas avec moi. Je vais te tuer.* Stay the fuck away from me and Anne."

Marc ends the call and leaves me in silence with this soul-crushing despair that is muted by denial.

This is the point where I finally lose it. I'm slipping, my sanity is less than existent, I need to get out of this cycle, I need to be able to know if people are here or not. I need to sober up.

I pick my phone back up, I'd dropped it--and tap a contact I've never called before, someone I am loath to ask for help, but I need it.

A dull and throaty voice answers my call, and as soon as she realizes who it is she drops the act.

"I'll be right there," she says.

There's no reason I'd ever call Laura, and she knows that, that's why she's so concerned. If I'm phoning her, something is wrong.

The panic and anxiety trickle down through my entire body from the very top of my head as I pace the house, waiting for her to get here. Beads of sweat are rolling off my face and this nauseous feeling is rising in my throat as my heart races, beating against my rib cage like it has some sort of vendetta against my system. Trembling, my hands make their way to the sides of my head, trying to steady the spinning.

When I finally lose the battle against gravity, when my knees give out beneath me, Laura is there to catch me. The tunnel vision is strong today.

"Hey, hey," Laura's voice rings through the haze of my panic, holding my weight and rubbing my back. "It's okay, it's alright, just breathe, I'm here."

For whatever reason, her shushing works. At least a little bit. My vision returns, the world stops spinning, my heart slows, but doesn't return to a normal rate. My chest still feels too tight.

"Tell me what's going on," she coos in a gentle, soothing voice. It's amazing to me how quickly her entire personality spins around from the crude, uncaring, self-hating witch that she normally is.

"I need to fix this, I need to get her back I can't..." when I look up at Laura's face, she's sporting an expression of calm understanding, but underneath her sympathy there's a sadness. That's what her self-destruction was; caring about somebody who would never love her. I close my eyes and shake my head a moment, trying to refocus on what's really important. "Luc is dead."

Her eyes grow wide, her eyebrows knit together in concern and a modicum of confusion. Her face is completely devoid of color. "Holy shit."

"I need to get clean," I know I'm not making sense, but there's a lot of things happening all at once and I can't differentiate one thing from another right now. I can't separate all of my emotions; I can't even fathom the idea that Luc isn't alive anymore. Why was she my first call?

Laura tells me to get into her car, and I do. The air is thick, and I'm having a hard time breathing. Time is passing so slowly that I can't actually tell if it's passing at all.

I need to be somewhere safe. I need to be somewhere that's completely dry. I need to be forced to stay sober, because all I want to do right now is go see Luc.

But I can't.

4

The blazing sun assaults all my senses as I sit out on too-fluffy furniture with the rest of the sketched-out people at this facility with me. It has some hopelessly optimistic name I can't be bothered to remember, and the people here, in this specific group, most of them are as early on in their journey to recovery as I am.

After a few days of sweating, shaking, dry heaving, and trying not to smash everything or cry for 10 hours straight, I'm exhausted. The only thing I have left to enjoy is smoking, which I've been doing constantly.

This monochromatic, yet dramatically bright world looks different through sober eyes. No longer am I seeing vibrant, colorful patterns or hope where there is none. What I'm seeing is that I am alone, and nothing is under my control, which I guess, technically, is the first step to recovery.

I've been listening to people's various sob stories about how they would get high under these sordid circumstances and how they neglected their lovers, their parents, their siblings, their kids, and how they wish they had been strong enough to overcome their addictions, how they wish they could have said 'no'. These people who are dutifully documenting their whole lives, assessing every action they made in the face of addiction, these people are not me, they are not like me.

Anna over there, she was just an alcoholic. She's sobbing now about how she used to scream at her kids when she had little to no patience for their whining. Leanne used to shoot up heroin. David had a problem with prescription grade painkillers, and Rob, he just really loved cocaine.

I guess technically even being here means that I'm on step four. I've already admitted that I have a problem, that I could restore my sanity by handing my strife over to a higher power.

All eyes are on me for a moment, and I wonder what I've missed. I haven't actually introduced myself to anybody here yet, so I guess they're waiting for that.

"Uhh, hi," I sputter, lifting a trembling hand to my lips so I can continue smoking my cigarette. There's no way in hell I'm giving my actual name to these people, and I figure a short version of my 'French' nickname is as good as any. "I'm Lou, and I'm an addict."

People on all sides of me mutter their greetings. The counsellor or whatever asks what's brought me to them today, what's my story, prompting the beginning of the next step.

"I've done a lot of questionable things in my life, but the thing is that through all of it I still had my own moral compass, as fucked up as it was," I laugh a little, punctuating the uncomfortable nature of this exchange. "Through my years of drug use and bullshit, one thing was constant: my relationship. And it took me fucking that up to even admit that I had a problem. She was always a saint about it." I take another long haul off my cigarette before continuing. "My drug of choice was always acid, and eventually that led to other things, more addictive things, but in the beginning, it was about altering my reality. I hated my life and I needed something beautiful to believe in. It wasn't real, none of it was real, but the colors, the concepts... everything is so beautiful when I'm tripping. But, as all things go, I fucked it up. I cheated on my fiancé because of my addiction, and that's ultimately what's brought me here, you know, I just want to be a better person. For her. She deserves it."

The counsellor looks at me like he knows something bigger is going on, but doesn't say anything else, and we move on to the next person.

After our little group therapy session, I stay outside. I'm a little way away from where we had all been sitting, still smoking obsessively. I need it now more than ever.

This gorgeous woman sidles up to me, taking a place at my side and pulls a cigarette out of my pack. I cast a glance at her as the sunlight plays off her long, wavy, blonde hair and deep, dark blue eyes.

"What happened the day that you came here?" she asks, nonchalantly, as though it weren't an incredibly intrusive question. I look at her, cocking an eyebrow for a moment before she bothers to elaborate. "You just seemed like so much more of an emotional mess than most of the people are when they first get here. Yeah, they're combative and frustrated and coming down and they want nothing more than to get more drugs, but you were... broken. So, what happened?"

"My best friend died."

"Is that why you're here?"

"I'm here because of my fiancé."

"We'll have fun with your relapse, then." Her voice is deep and sensual. She doesn't have Laura's vocal fry, nor does she have Liache's singsong tones, but something wholly unique. It's comfortable, like she was just born to bathe people in inner peace.

"Who the fuck are you?" I ask, probably coming off like a total jerk.

"Dylan. And I want to help you, if you'll let me."

I don't respond, just look out with her at the beautiful landscape of this facility. I wonder idly how much this is costing the record label.

"How old were you when you started?" she asks, pointedly.

"16," I answer sluggishly before taking another long drag off the cigarette between my fingers. "Didn't take me long."

"Apparently."

"Well once you find the drug supply in your town, you can pretty much get anything."

"Don't I know it." Dylan laughs. "What started it?"

"I was bored." I think about this for a moment, figuring she's trying to get me to do that chronicling thing, search my morals. "It was boring, life back then. Nothing fun ever happened. I was just starting to play with the idea of music, just starting to write these terrible, angsty lyrics. It was awful, but everything seemed so much better when I was high. Before long, I realized that life was more beautiful, more meaningful when I was hallucinating, and shit just escalated from there. Gabriel just watched it happen, he never did anything to stop me back then. I guess he thought I'd grow out of it or some shit."

Dylan grabs another cigarette out of my pack and lights it, eventually holding the filter out to my lips. "Now we're sharing spit, too."

Despite myself, I smile. "I don't like how easy this is for

you. What's your angle?"

"I just thought it was high time you started in on that fourth step. Keep talking, killer," she giggles. "More about the music thing. That sounds like a story."

I scoff. "Not really. Typical bullshit story. I started a band with Gabriel when we were teenagers, we just played like shit in my basement until we got better, and we found two other guys to play with us. Really it was just me screaming at the top of my lungs until something stuck."

"So, when did the fiancé come in?"

"Right at the end of senior year. She was younger, I want to say she was a sophomore."

"Seriously?" Dylan's thin compassionate act drops at once out of frustration. "High school sweethearts? What fuckin' century is this?"

"Hey, it's not like there weren't girls before her," I sputter in defense. "They just weren't mine. They weren't for me. She's for me."

Her eyes narrow as she hauls off her own cigarette, a skeptical tone seeping into her voice. "Alright... what exactly does that mean?"

"It means nobody else stood out." It means that about ten years ago, I walked away from Michelle or Ashley or whatever her name was, and up to Liache and asked her out. It means that those first few fucks weren't anything important, they were just what they were.

There was a time before Liache, but I can't really remember it. My life only really began when we all got together, when I met Liache. She was so cute with her loosely curled pigtails and braces. She was young and hopeful, and she seemed to glow, she stood out from the crowd. The first thing I noticed were her eyes, emerald green and standing out from the backdrop of blonde hair and blue eyes, standing out from the parade of black dye and eyeliner of every other girl that threw herself at me.

And when I asked her out, she said no.

She said that she knew better.

She said that she'd heard about me. And I smiled at her.

She peered around me and looked at the characterless girl

I'd just left behind. "And who's she?"

I waved my hand dismissively, never taking my eyes off Liache. "Unimportant."

Finally, she cracked a bit of a smile as the clone girl stomped off, muttering about what an asshole I was. "You get one date," Liache said.

Dylan's voice pulls me out of my reminiscing abruptly. "Still with me?"

I drop my gaze from the landscape to the ground below us, smiling bashfully to myself. "Yeah," I say before taking another long haul off my cigarette. "So, what about you, oh master of mystery? Why are you here?"

"Oh no." Dylan laughs and flashes a blinding smile at me. "This isn't about me. This is all you, champ."

As she turns and walks away, I can't help but notice her perfectly sculpted ass. The bounce in her step, the way her hips sway, the way she glances back over her shoulder at me, and winks tells me that this was on purpose, and I almost want to follow her.

But not today.

"It's been a week, and nobody has come to visit me, and I can't say I blame them." I find myself in a group session, opening up. It doesn't mean that I'm identifying with these people, but it means that at the very least, I'm sorting through my own shit. "They all have their own lives and I think that my selfish bullshit finally wore thin, and honestly, I'm glad if they've moved on. They deserve to be happy.

"This whole 'searching moral inventory' thing is dangerous for me because if I look back and take an accurate look at everything, I realize that everything I've ever done has really been all about myself, about my self-loathing, or my addiction. And that really sucks because I always thought that I was trying to make money to support my girlfriend, but it was really about keeping her around, dragging her into my downward spiral of dog shit."

In my spare time, I've been compiling a list of the people I've hurt. It's limited to the people closest to me, only because I never really cared about or interacted with anybody who wasn't in my inner circle. It takes a certain level of egotism to only notice the people you interact with every day, to only care about four people in the entire world. I've probably fucked up a lot of fans, a lot of people who for whatever reason looked up to me, and that weighs heavily on my conscience right now. There's a whole huge group of people that I won't be able to make amends to.

After the group session, I meet with Liache in the lobby. She's the only one who cares, and for obvious reasons. She's not ready to let me go, but at this point I'm convinced that it's what she needs to do. It doesn't matter if she's my guardian angel, she deserves better than what I can provide for her.

"You look like shit," she says as I walk up to her. She wraps her arms around me in a tight hug and takes a step back.

Looking her over, I realize she's dressed from head to toe in black. Maybe it's the outfit, but she looks more monotone, more drab to me than usual. "Is it today?" I ask.

She nods. "You should come. It would be good for you."

"I don't think it would be good for Marc, though."

"Well, the people who matter know it's not your fault." Liache shifts uncomfortably where she stands, tucking a few loose strands of her hair behind her ear. "Gabriel and me, we don't blame you."

"Yeah," I mutter, mulling over the idea that she still lives under his roof, with him. Even though I've seen her room clearly being lived in, even though I've seen the evidence, I still can't help but to feel self-conscious. She lives with fucking Hercules.

From behind me, heavy footsteps announce the arrival of a new acquaintance of mine. A flash of blonde hair and a too-friendly smile seem to materialize on my right.

"Is this the fiancé?" Dylan asks, too eagerly. "You didn't tell me she was so pretty, Lou."

Liache's eyes meet mine, her eyebrows raise in an incredulous glance as she shakes Dylan's outstretched hand. She mouths the nickname back at me, questioning me.

I clear my throat. "Yes, this is the fiancé. Fiancé, this is Dylan. Dylan, this is—"

"Lilly. It's nice to meet you."

I laugh despite myself at Liache's improvised name. She must have figured out that I never gave my real name.

"It's nice to meet you too," Dylan says, her words dripping with simulated sweetness. "It's good to have a face to go with the stories."

"Oh?" The surprise is clear in Liache's voice. The way she glances over at me is like a warning shot.

"I've been helping Lou work the steps." Poison drips from Dylan's plastic smile. Her friendliness is poorly glued to a far less personable, but more genuine motive. I see what she's doing, it's something I've done to myself for months now. I've been spending so much time convincing myself of her infidelity that I never even considered that somebody would plant the seed of mine in her head.

Dylan isn't being friendly, nor is she being insincere. Every move, every flirtatious glance, every too-sweet smile is calculated. It's actually beautiful from a twisted and broken point of view. Her act draws me in, and I find myself staring slack-jawed at their exchange.

Liache turns to face me. "Well, I'm glad that you're making friends." Her arms are stiff at her sides, and her tone has sharpened, as though she's scolding me. She's jealous and she's trying to hide it, but the blush in her face gives her away. "I have to go to your best friend's funeral, so if you're not coming…"

Dylan interjects, "I'm not actually sure that would be the best thing for his sobriety…"

I shake my head, floored by Dylan's brazen remarks. Marc would murder me on the spot, I can't do that to him, to his parents.

"Alright. Whatever. I'll be back to talk to you tomorrow. It was nice to meet you, Dylan." She doesn't give her a chance to respond, stalking off into the bright outdoors without another word.

I hate knowing that Liache is upset, but I'm intrigued by Dylan's motive. Her pure malice is intoxicating, and I'm more than a little amused by the exchange.

"What the hell was that?" I ask with a wide, mischievous

grin of my own.

"Oh, that?" Dylan asks. "I was fucking with her."

"Why?" My curiosity is burning through what feels like all my synapses.

"Same reason you both gave me fake names," Dylan replies simply. "I fucking can."

I'm blown away by her in this moment. I have spent so long in my own life hating myself and knowing that I manipulate people to get what I want that it is easy to recognize that she does the exact same thing. The difference is that she revels in it. She uses it, molds it, and takes delight in it.

And for the first time, I'm second guessing my entire relationship.

"A month since the funeral," I mutter in our group session. It's obvious to everybody here that I've been stewing in my shitty emotions ever since. "Nobody, not one person has reached out to me." I can't bring myself to make the call. It feels like defeat. "And I know it's not about me, I don't expect the bereaved to make a fucking appearance, but she's supposed to care about me."

Blank looks from everybody around. Nobody knows how to react. Fucking useless.

We aren't outside today so I can't just light up a cigarette and I might as well be suffocating. No drugs, no cigarettes, no Liache.

The sound of my shoe squeaking on the floor with every bounce of my knee reverberates back from the walls as some other person drones on about their problems. I'm restless, I can't stop my knee from bouncing, my entire body is crawling with an energy I can barely control, and I hate every fucking second of it.

My school chair clatters to the ground as I stand abruptly and leave the room, headed for outside. I don't care what anybody else has to say and I can't think straight anyway. The hot, bitter taste of smoke crawls down my throat and up my nose when I light up. This is the one remaining addiction I have, and I am not strong enough to give it up. I need something to destroy myself with, I need one last vestige of slow, methodical suicide.

"Having a rough day?" Dylan's voice floats through the air, massaging my eardrums with sultry vibrations. She hasn't made this any easier.

Dylan has crawled into my head and made herself a nest. She has invaded my every thought and tainted everything I thought I knew. I should have been reaching out to Liache, I shouldn't leave everything on her shoulders, but if I really wanted to talk to her, if I really wanted to feel like she cared, wouldn't I have done that already? What's stopping me?

"You could say that," I scoff. This woman is everywhere, in everything I do, and I'm irritated by it. I want nothing more right now than to get high, forget what gravity is, forget my own name and lose myself, but I can't.

"Talk to me," she urges, but it feels like prying.

"I shouldn't have bothered coming here," I confess. "I should have cut my losses and moved on. But she told me I still had a shot, so I had to take it." I've convinced myself that she's started seeing Gabriel again, she must have. There's no other logical reason for me to believe she would distance herself like this.

"Stop doing this for her," Dylan coos quietly, sliding too closely beside me. "This journey isn't about her, it's about you. Work on yourself."

The scent of her surrounds me. It's nostalgic, like the smell of the beach. Like sunscreen, sea air, sand, and coconut all at the same time. It's fresh and light, and somehow, I'm still drowning in it.

She hooks her pinky in mine. "Be selfish," she says.

A lopsided smirk graces my face before I pull my hand away. She's right, and I know she's right. She said it from the beginning, if I'm doing this for her then I'm going to relapse. Right now, I'm not sure if it's worth the struggle. Today has been hard enough and the only reason I'm sober is because the facility is dry. Completely dry.

"I would kill for a hit of literally anything right now." It feels good to admit that in this moment.

"I know," she says quietly. "And that's okay."

I am overwhelmed. The ebb and flow of emotions

coursing through my body is too much to bear. I fucking hate it, but I trust her. I don't realize I'm crying until a tear rolls off my nose and onto the pavement below.

"This sucks," I mutter after several breaths. "How do people do this?"

Dylan laughs gently, reaching for my hands. "They don't usually try to go it alone."

I'm not looking at her, my eyes are still fixed to that spot on the ground, where my tears are pooling and forcing me to confront them. She rests her forehead against mine and her warmth seems to spread through me from there. I've never felt more open, more naked, more free or completely pathetic in my life. Yes, I trust her, but why?

My friendship, my every relationship comes with a level of distrust, paranoia. My oldest friends, my fiancé, everybody has some plan for betrayal in my mind. Gabriel, Luc, even Liache. Dylan's motives seem clear and straightforward. She is easy to read and wears her heart on her sleeve. She may have intentions, but at least they're clear ones.

Her hands slide up my arms and over my shoulders to cradle my face. She guides my chin gently up and plants a soft kiss on my lips. Her warmth is so inviting, the physical touch is comforting, and I find myself kissing her back despite knowing it's not good for me right now.

"Oh, shit," Laura's voice comes floating on the too-humid air to pull me out of this emotional well. "Sorry, I can come back."

Dylan chuckles slightly as she pulls away from me. "No, it's fine. I think we're done here." She walks away and leaves me stranded with a mess of emotions that I'm not sure how to process.

When I look over at Laura, her face is screwed up in a scowl. "That girl is just a giant red flag," she says, circling her hand in the air toward Dylan and then turning her gaze toward me. "What the hell do you think you're doing?"

I laugh, a little too hard, while wiping the tears from my face. "Not a fucking clue."

"Are you crying?" she asks, incredulous. "I didn't think

I'd ever have to see you cry again, I'm not sure how to handle it anymore." She slides her sunglasses up over her forehead, placing them firmly on top of her head and plops down on a nearby sofa.

"Fuck you, Laura," I say, cracking a smile. I sit beside her and light a cigarette off the butt of the last one, then stamp the old one out in an ashtray. "Why are you here?"

She gapes at me in mock surprise. "Do I need a reason to be here?"

"Nobody enters a rehab facility without a reason."

"Fair point." She sighs heavily. "I wanted to check on you. See how you were doing. You weren't at the funeral and Liache was…"

"Gorgeous?" I inquire hopefully.

"Testy. To say the least."

"She met Dylan before she went." I take a long haul off my cigarette, this isn't a conversation I'm particularly ready for but it's the one I'm having. I inhale deeply, then speak with my voice muffled through the thick smoke. "She said she was going to come back to talk to me the next day and never did."

"The blonde is probably why." She takes my cigarette from my hand, takes a drag, then gives it back. "You not going was a super bad look, by the way."

"I couldn't do that…"

"To Marc, I know," she interrupts. "He's made no secret of wanting you dead, but still. It's not a great look."

This isn't helping my mood today. "Why are you here?" I ask again, my tone dull and monotonous. "A month later, why did you finally deem this appropriate?" Anger bubbles just below the surface of my calm facade.

"I needed to know you were okay, but I couldn't bring myself to come out here," she blurts, a little too loudly, in reaction to the anger in my own tone. "Is that what you want to hear?" She's fully facing me, all but yelling in my face. And I deserve it. "I couldn't come out here because I fucking love you for some ridiculous ass reason and seeing you in pieces like you were when I brought you here wasn't an option for me." She laughs, in near hysterics. "Fuck, coming out here and seeing you in tears making out with some rando wasn't an option for me

105

either but here we are."

"I'm sorry," I mutter quietly. "I'm so sorry, I know our relationship isn't, it never was something normal and I owe you an apology for that."

"I knew what I was getting into, but I appreciate the sentiment." She lights her own cigarette and looks out over the balcony, clearly deep in thought. "I don't want you like I did, because it wasn't good for either of us, but I do want to be your friend because I care about you despite myself. You're a piece of shit but nobody has ever gotten me like you do."

I laugh. "Nobody else can see through your transparent wall?"

"Nobody ever cared enough to try." The end of her cigarette lights up and crackles as she takes another drag. Smoke curls around her features, highlighting her specific brand of beauty and disappears into the ether.

I lace my fingers through hers. "We can try this platonic friend thing, and I promise not to hate you too much."

She smiles. "Definitely no telling me how much I disgust you or I may not be able to control myself." She leans forward and stamps out her cigarette butt. "I have to go. I'm glad you're okay and I won't wait so long to visit again."

I run my thumb gently back and forth over hers. "Thank you for coming out today, I wasn't doing too great. It's nice to have someone who cares."

"Don't be too hard on Gabriel and Liache," she says, a sympathetic look gracing her features. "They're still healing, too."

It's hard for me to remember that I'm not the center of the universe, that other people have their own feelings and thoughts and that sometimes I'm a paranoid prick.

We stand, I give her a quick hug and she goes on her way, leaving me to deal with whatever the hell has been happening here. Of course, she's probably right, Dylan is probably just one, gigantic red flag I should be avoiding, but it's just so hard when she is everywhere here.

I stare out over the darkening balcony as the sun sets, my mind swirling with absolute confusion as I have a moment now to myself to process.

I've been here for just over a month and I've formed what feels to be a solid bond with another human being, one not tied to my sordid past, who appears, for all intents and purposes, to have my best interest at heart. She talked me through my worst moment here, kissed me, and then left.

What the hell is her game?

Halfway through a 90-day program isn't somewhere I ever thought I'd be, and it's certainly not a place I ever wanted to be.

This place is worse than purgatory at this point.

Laura has been checking up to make sure I'm drying out alright, making sure I'm on track for the record label. They want a tour pretty much immediately after I leave this place and I must admit I would rather that than anything else right now.

I'm still trying to do better by Laura, trying to show her that I do care about her as a human being, despite my first impression. It's fortuitous that she was put in my path, regardless of the fallout from our first encounter. She's an amazing friend. She has also been bringing me cigarettes which is a good thing since I am going through them faster than I previously thought humanly possible.

I still haven't heard a word from Liache, and I still can't get a read on Dylan. I've been stewing in my own paranoia, too afraid to call Liache and hear that she has indeed left me for Gabriel and all the emotions that I didn't get the chance to address with Dylan. It's obvious to me that there's some level of chemistry, but I'm not sure to what end she's chasing it. Is she even chasing it? I wouldn't even be fully convinced she existed if I weren't sober. But I am, so she must.

Right?

It is mid-afternoon, and I am sprawled out in the sunshine, chain-smoking as always when Dylan manifests herself from the shadows.

"It's been a minute," I say, not bothering to cast a full glance her way.

"I do that."

I squint at her from my reclined position on this outdoor sofa, my hand blocking the sun along my brow. "So, what the fuck?"

She laughs. "Yeah, I do that too."

I sit forward, frustration bubbling up from the depths of my soul. "No, seriously," I implore. "What the fuck? You kissed me and then ghosted."

"She still hasn't called you, huh?"

"Fucking forgets about her!" I shout into the minimal distance between us. "I asked you a question, Dylan. You. What are you doing?"

"Deflecting."

"Why?"

"Because this isn't about me."

"Yes, it is, stop that." Annoyance is seeping out through my seams; my tone is sharp and short. "I don't do this; I don't talk to people. I don't open up. You got in past my walls then you disappeared."

She doesn't say anything, she won't even look at me and I'm left to search the air between us for some hint of meaning. All I can focus on is how annoyed I am by life in general right now. I never thought I would have anybody but Liache to depend on, and right now I'm faced with someone I thought I could trust, but clearly can't.

"We need to talk about what happened." My voice is shaky, tears are welling up behind my eyes despite myself. I feel disconnected from the emotions I'm displaying, disconnected from the person I thought I was.

"One kiss?" she scoffs at me. The words leave a wound behind I didn't expect.

"Is that it?" I ask. "Is that really it? Because to me, it feels like you worked awfully hard to get my trust before that kiss. It felt like you were trying to get closer. It felt like you gave a shit about me."

"So, a woman has to be in love with you to care about you as a human being?" She laughs. "Get over yourself."

I am stunned. I can feel it written all over my face, and I don't know what to say. It takes me a second to collect my thoughts. I rise to my feet and look down at her in her chair. "I don't know what game you're playing, but I'm out. I'm not going to sit here and argue semantics with you over who kissed whom. I'm done." I take a few steps away and tell her, "I don't even know you."

I'm the king of projection. I am an unreliable human being. I am not made to be here, dealing with these people, and that's why it's such an effective punishment. That's why God has put me here in His infinite wisdom. I am my own worst enemy. He doesn't have to torture me; I do that myself. Must be fucking nice.

Quick footsteps echo down the hall behind me as I approach the door to my room. I open it and find myself being pushed inside and shoved against the nearest wall.

"Listen here, you narcissistic ass," Dylan hisses through her teeth as the door slams shut behind us. "You're not the only person here who has shit going on."

I laugh. Her face is barely an inch from mine, and I can't care less that I am laughing in her face. She slaps me, and the sound hangs in the air for a moment before I take several steps forward, making her step back and tumble back onto my bed. "No hitting."

She glowers at me but doesn't even try to move as I pin her hands down to the bed. I hover above her, not letting our bodies touch while she glares directly into my eyes. I don't know what her problem is today, but this is surprisingly hot.

"Now, tell me," I coo quietly into her ear. "Why would you want to hurt me with all those things you said today? Do you really think I am that self-centered? That I wouldn't care about something you're going through?"

Her gaze softens, but she says nothing.

"You worked so damn hard to get on my good side, did you think you were disposable to me?" I sigh slightly, studying her face. The way her blonde hair frames her features, how her eyes are such a deep, dark blue that they look bottomless. "Here I was worried you'd disappeared because you didn't care about me, and it looks like you were scared I didn't care about you."

"Do you?" she asks as a tear rolls silently down the side

of her face.

I've never been on this side of reassurance before. It feels odd, but not forced. Not now, not with her. I let go of her hand to wipe away her tears. "I do," I tell her. She seemed so strong before, so impassive. I wonder if it was all just a show, or if her focus on my issues helped to mask her own.

She leans up just slightly, breaching the short distance between our faces, and kisses me, passionately. It is gentle, but insistent and before we are fully aware of it, we are feverishly working to strip each other.

This time, there's some privacy, no Laura to walk in, nothing to interrupt as the dam breaks, as my fingers explore the curve of her breasts, every fold of her body, every exquisite inch of her being. I am enthralled by watching her react, the rise of the blush in her cheeks, the thin sheen of sweat that makes her skin glisten in the afternoon light flooding in from behind the thin parchment blinds.

We try our hardest to stay quiet, privacy is difficult to come by even at this glorified hotel the record label has put me in. The heavy breathing, the sharp gasps, and stifled moans raise the intensity and our excitement skyrockets with each desperate move.

I am lost in the chaos, drowning in her scent and intoxicated by her very existence, unable to admit to myself that this was something I wanted from the beginning. She buries her fingers in my hair and pulls, sending me over the edge before she collapses onto me, recovering from her own tumble into oblivion. Every moment of this has been exquisite, hot and urgent, and very needed. For a moment, I forget everything that's been swimming in my head since I got here, for just one moment I get to exist in the present.

Lying in bed with her feels strange, iniquitous, yet deliciously so. The forbidden fruit in the garden of Eden, only I'm the one being tempted this time.

As my thoughts begin to creep back and swirl around my mind, I decide that it serves Liache right. At least this time. She insisted I come here, and then she left me to my own devices while she continued to live with Gabriel. I'm not really upset anymore, because I'm no longer in rehab for her. I'm doing it for me. I deserve better. I deserve to live.

"I'm sorry I was such an asshole," Dylan mutters quietly from my shoulder. "I'm not so good with processing emotions and, you know, being a functional human being."

I laugh. "Me neither." I wrap my arms around her and kiss her forehead gently. This feels good, this feels constructive, it feels easy. "I'm going to venture to guess that might be why we're both here."

"Fair assumption." She sighs as she stands and gets dressed.

"Will you be disappearing for weeks again?" I laugh, not entirely sure if I'm meaning to make a joke or if my feelings are still hurt. This has been an odd exchange, even for me.

"Maybe."

The next day and I have a visitor. I'm not thrilled about the experience, and I wasn't expecting to feel this incredibly fucking angry about it. I thought I'd moved on from my suspicions, but this is the first time that Gabriel has considered it appropriate to visit me.

He approaches me, almost looking like he's expecting a hug, and upon seeing the look on my face decides that is probably not the best idea. He's not wrong. I'm barely holding my anger and I'm sure it's obvious in the lack of expression on my face.

"Why are you here?" I spit the words like venom at his feet.

"Are you fucking serious right now?" He sighs, brushing his hair out of his face with both hands. "I could have sworn we put this to bed ages ago."

"So, what, are you gonna tell me I'm crazy?" I laugh slightly through my nose. "Or are you here to break some news?"

There's a hesitation in his demeanor suddenly. He is hiding something. I knew it. "You need to call Liache."

I scoff. "So, she can tell me that you two will live happily ever after without me? No thanks."

"Do you have to be so fucking stubborn? I swear if you two got any more alike you'd share a brain." His frustration is palpable. "I don't know why I need to tell you this, but I'm gay, man. I don't have any interest in her and even if I did, I'd never do that to you." He scoffs, "I've introduced you to like, five of my boyfriends."

A lot of things clicked into place at that moment. And he was right, he shouldn't have needed to do this, especially at this moment for this reason. I'm not as all-knowing as I think I am. I'm so forgetful, so self-absorbed that I can't even remember something this important.

"It hurts me that you think I'd do that to you."

"Fuck." The word falls from my lips. "I'm an asshole."

Gabriel laughs. "Yeah, you are."

There are several moments of complete silence between us during which I mull over why I'm feeling so jealous, so protective, and so volatile. None of this should matter. I'm toxic, I'm possessive, I'm a monster.

"I'm gonna tell Liache to call you." His tone is quieter, more gentle now. "You two really need to talk."

"Is she okay?"

Gabriel laughs. "She's... she's fine. And I don't know what you have going on here but I think you need to figure yourself out before you do something you can't undo."

It is another several days of silence. I spend it alone, in my room, avoiding the group sessions, the prying eyes, the newbies coming in and the people graduating from the program. I don't want to be faced with my stagnation. I don't want to do anything but process myself. I sit and I think about my reactions to Gabriel over the months, the mistakes I have made with Laura, with Liache, with Dylan. I've been having nightmares about Luc. His parents, his brother. I've barely slept. I need to get it together, I need to stop the body count.

Nightmares where I'm alone in the abyss, nothing exists except for me and the blackness. Then there's fire, and then Luc. And he's consumed by it. Tongues of the flames lick forth from his eyes, from his mouth, from the tips of his fingers and toes and he cackles and it echoes inside my head. And I hear it every moment of every day, echoing through eternity. I stop sleeping.

And Dylan is nowhere to be found. Again.

I'm outside chain-smoking an entire pack of cigarettes when Gabriel walks up with Liache. She looks furious. She looks beautiful, she looks perfect and amazing. She's grace incarnate. She starts talking to me and I barely hear what she has to say. Her anger turns to concern as she studies my face, and she reaches out to touch my cheek. She turns to Gabriel and says something but I'm having a hard time concentrating.

"Hey!" Gabriel's voice cuts through the fog. "Are you okay?"

I laugh. "Livin' the dream, buddy."

Gabriel and Liache share a concerned glance. I'm just along for the ride at this point. I can't believe that I'm so insufficient, that I can't be left alone for more than five minutes without completely falling apart.

Before I realize what's happening, I've been ushered into her bed at Gabriel's and am slipping from consciousness.

I dream that I'm back in my abyss, that fire is consuming me from the inside out, my skin bubbles and blisters and flames burst forth from the open sores. I wake abruptly in a sweat and look at my hands and arms. They're steaming. I scoff quietly to myself as I realize my body may be having trouble containing my damned soul running on such little sleep.

The sleep I have had here has done me well. I look around and breathe the air, and it feels so different from the facility. Fresher, lighter, cleaner.

Liache peeks her head in the room. "Oh, you're awake." It's a treat to hear her sweet, clear voice again. It's not angry, it's not frustrated, it is relieved.

"Yeah," I reply. "I guess I needed that."

I lean back against the pillows as she sits on the edge of the bed. She smiles gently and holds my hand, but says nothing.

"Hey," I say quietly, trying to get her to raise her eyes to meet mine. "Are you alright?"

She sighs. "Yeah, I..." she pauses, unsure how to move forward. Concern rises in my chest, threatening to pull me into a panic. Nobody will tell me what's happening with her, and I'm starting to get scared.

"You know you can tell me anything, right?" It's meant to be
comforting but comes off as pleading. "I've fucked everything up enough for the both of us, I won't judge you for any stupid thing."

She laughs and pauses again. "I'm pregnant."

Made in the USA
Middletown, DE
07 October 2022